P9-EGN-385

32,078

M   Ferrars, E.X.
        Thinner than water.

DATE	ISSUED TO
APR 2 6 1982	77-152
MAY 7 1982	77-404
JUN 1 2 1982	77-559
JUL 2 1982	77-032
JUL 2 2 1982	78-1086
JUL 2 9 1982	77-116
AUG 1 8 1982	77-442
MAY 2 6 1985	77-113

Mynderse Public Library
Seneca Falls, N. Y.

By F. X. Ferrars

Thinner Than Water

Thinner Than Water

E. X. FERRARS

PUBLISHED FOR THE CRIME CLUB BY

DOUBLEDAY & COMPANY, INC.

GARDEN CITY, NEW YORK

1982

32,078

All of the characters in this book
are fictitious, and any resemblance
to actual persons, living or dead,
is purely coincidental.

MYNDERSE LIBRARY
31 Fall Street
Seneca Falls, New York 13148

Library of Congress Cataloging in Publication Data

Ferrars, E. X.
Thinner than water.

I. Title.
PR6003.R458T5   1982   823'.912
ISBN 0-385-17946-4   AACR2
Library of Congress Catalog Card Number 81-43393
Copyright © 1982 by M. D. Brown
All Rights Reserved
Printed in the United States of America
First Edition in the United States of America

Thinner Than Water

CHAPTER 1

When I came up the moving stairs and emerged into the roundabout at Piccadilly underground station and a man who was passing took me in his arms and kissed me warmly, I thought to myself, "I believe I must have met this man before." But casual kissing has become so general as a form of greeting that it seemed to me possible that whoever it was and I had chatted for only five minutes at somebody's party and had never even known each other's names.

Then my vision, or rather my mind, cleared and I exclaimed, "Gavin!"

"I thought for a moment you hadn't recognized me," he said.

"Of course I did."

But the truth was that Gavin Brownlow had changed a great deal since I had seen him last. But that had been something like five years ago, if I remembered correctly. At any rate it had been on an occasion when, over lunch, he had wanted my advice as to whether or not he and his wife, Kay, should go ahead with a divorce. That had been a year or so after I and my husband, Felix, had parted, and it had appeared that Gavin had thought that my experience in such matters might be helpful to him.

Not that he had really wanted advice. He had only wanted to talk to someone who, he could feel fairly secure, would not think of offering him any. And actually Felix and I had never had a divorce. We had simply gone our separate ways, the strange episode of our marriage seeming so unreal that there had been no necessity for us to suffer the trauma of going through divorce proceedings. That had happened about six years ago. So according to the calculations that went through my head rapidly as Gavin and I stood embraced in the underground, it must have been about five years since we had last met.

He was still as handsome as ever, but his black hair had turned grey, though he could not have been more than forty, and it had altered his appearance almost as much as a new hat can alter that of a woman. His face had grown thinner too, which gave him a faintly haggard air of maturity, and as he stood back from me and looked me over I saw that he stooped slightly, as if he spent too much of his time at an office desk. He went to a good tailor, too, which was something that he had never bothered about in the old days. However, he still had his likeable air of vagueness and of wanting someone to be kind to him and take care of him.

"What are you doing?" he asked. "Are you very busy? Could we have lunch together?"

I was only in London for the day to do some shopping and I was already bored with it. The crowds were getting on my nerves and I had failed to find any of the things I wanted. As I always did each time I came to London nowadays, I had been making up my mind that in future I should do all my shopping in the small town where I live. So I told Gavin that I should love to have lunch with him. It was just what was needed to save my day from having been a total waste of time.

"We'll go to Fecino's then," he said.

That was pure sentimentality. Fecino's was the small restaurant in Dean Street where he and Kay and Felix and I used to meet for lunch or dinner on the rare occasions when one of us had had enough money for it, in the days when we were all happily married. On the whole I would sooner have gone somewhere else, but if it was where Gavin wanted to go,

I did not feel like objecting. We went up the stairs into Shaftesbury Avenue and walked along towards Dean Street.

The pavements were too crowded for us to be able to talk as we went, but once we were settled at a table in the restaurant and had ordered drinks, Gavin gave me one of his direct yet curiously diffident looks and said, "Well, tell me how things are with you, Virginia. Have you stuck to that physiotherapy thing?"

I said I had.

"And that satisfies you?"

"I can think of more exciting ways of earning a living," I said, "but I'm not qualified to do anything else and it really suits me very well. It's part time and I don't have to work frightfully hard. What about you?"

"Oh, I've gone into the family firm in Spellbridge, as I always knew I should in the end," he answered. "We're Brownlow and Son nowadays."

"Your father hasn't retired?"

"Not yet. He talks about it sometimes, but in fact he'll go on till he drops."

Gavin and his father were both architects. When Gavin had been younger he had looked down on his father's work and had had ambitions to set up on his own, as far away as possible from the depressing Midland town where he had grown up. But, with middle age approaching, a secure and comfortable income might have acquired greater attractions than it had had in his youth. His father, I knew, was financially a very successful man.

"Do you get on better with each other than you used to?" I asked.

"Oh yes, we get on pretty well," Gavin answered. "I've even moved in with him and Hannah. You remember Hannah?"

I remembered her dimly. I had met her only two or three times. She was Gavin's younger sister and was almost as good-looking as he was, but had been a shy, rather prickly young woman.

"She hasn't married?" I said.

"No, she's always stayed at home and run the house for my father. I've tried to get her away from him for her own good, but she only seems to resent it. And he's pretty possessive where she's concerned. What about you? You haven't married again?"

I shook my head. Our drinks had come and the waiter had thrust large menus into our hands. I hoped that Gavin would decide what I should like to eat, as I like most things and large menus always intimidate me.

He studied his with what was apparently concentration, but what he said next had nothing to do with it.

"That's what I'm going to do myself," he said.

"Get married again?" The information did not surprise me. The surprising thing really was that it had not happened sooner.

"Yes, next week," he said. "That's why I'm in London. I'm buying a present for her. I suppose . . ." He hesitated, then gave me one of his bright, shy smiles. "I suppose I can't persuade you to come along and help me choose it. I'm simply no good at that kind of thing."

"I don't think I am either, and as I don't even know her, I'll be quite useless," I said. "But I'll come and look on if it'll help to give you self-confidence. What's it going to be? Diamonds?"

"No, not diamonds. I gave diamonds to Kay."

I had never known what he had felt about his divorce from Kay.

"Whom are you marrying?" I asked. "Tell me about her."

But at that point the waiter intervened and I remembered that Gavin was one of the people who have to have their food chosen for them, so after all I had to take the responsibility for it and helped him to order vichyssoise and blanquette de veau for us both and a bottle of Gewürztraminer.

After that I said again, "Tell me about her, Gavin."

"Her name's Rosie," he said. "Rosalind, which I much prefer, though Rosie suits her somehow. Rosie Flint. The Flints are neighbours of ours. They run a sort of market garden and Rosie's father, Oliver, does all sorts of other things too, paints a bit and takes wonderful photographs, and I believe he's written a novel too, though I don't think it had much notice taken of it. You probably know that sort of person. Lots of talent . . . I don't think anything he's done has ever quite come off, but he's a very interesting chap. I think her mother, Nora, is really the backbone of the family."

"But I was asking you about Rosie, not her parents," I said.

"Oh yes, well, I don't know quite how to describe her." He blushed slightly. "In my view she's exceptionally lovely and very intelligent, too. She got a first in social science at University College, but she never parades that, and she's wonderfully alive, but gentle, too. . . . Oh, hell, how does one describe a girl one's in love with?"

"I suppose it's rather difficult."

"The trouble is . . ."

Of course there was bound to be trouble. Gavin, apart from his work, at which I had always had the impression that he was notably gifted, was a most incompetent person who could find his way into trouble even when there seemed to be no possible risk of it.

"Yes?" I said.

"She's only twenty-three and I'm nearly forty."

"Seventeen years," I said. "Well, I shouldn't worry too much about it. You're wearing very well. People don't age as rapidly as they used to."

"But don't you realize that when she's only fifty I'll be approaching seventy?"

"I'm glad you're thinking so far ahead. That must be a good sign."

"Do you really think so?" He looked bashfully pleased. "When you've once made the sort of hash of things that I did with Kay, you feel pretty scared of trying again. But yes, I think you're right, I think it's going to work out this time."

"After all, Kay's a rather difficult person, isn't she?" I said. "I've always been fond of her, but I've always thought one would have to be very strong-minded to live with her day in, day out."

"That's the truth. And I was only just strong-minded enough to step back from the brink before it was too late. D'you know, I don't know what I might have done if I'd gone on living with her. But I'll tell you something, Virginia. One of the things I've always been grateful to you for was that you never took sides when things between Kay and me were coming apart. Most people did, my father and Hannah, for instance. They didn't understand Kay and they were entirely on her side, which actually didn't help her or me in the least. But thinking about all that has just given me an idea. I think it's a rather splendid idea. . . ."

He was interrupted by the waiter returning and putting our bowls of vichyssoise before us.

Felix has told me since then that that was when I should have started to feel apprehensive. He has claimed that if only I had remembered how badly most of Gavin's good ideas turned out I should have saved myself a great deal of distress and trouble. That, however, is the sort of thing that it is very easy to say after an event. Felix has always been strong on hindsight. It can sometimes make him sound very wise. But I am sure there was no reason at the time why I should have felt anything but a mild curiosity about Gavin's splendid idea. As he and I started on our soup I waited for him to go on.

He gave me a warm smile. "How would you like to be a

witness at the wedding?" he asked. "You were a witness when Kay and I were married and you're one of my oldest friends. I do wish you'd do it."

"Yes, Felix and I were the witnesses, weren't we?" I said. "I'd hardly call that a good omen for the second time around."

"Please do it," he said. "You always give me a sort of feeling of security and I need that quite badly at the moment. You see, almost everybody is against this marriage, partly because of the age difference and partly because I'm divorced. Nora Flint likes me, I think, but I know she had her heart set on a church affair for Rosie, with bridesmaids and all, but our vicar won't hear of that, and my father dislikes the whole Flint family because he despises everything they care about, and Hannah is always against everything I do. I don't think Oliver's against it, but he's totally indifferent to the whole affair and doesn't care what happens as long as he's left in peace. So if only you'd come I'd feel I'd got at least one friend to back me up."

"It's going to be at a registrar's, is it?"

"Yes, in Spellbridge. And then perhaps after it you and Felix and Rosie and I could have lunch together and go on afterwards to the reception Nora has set her heart on. I'd prefer it if Rosie and I could just go away quietly after we'd signed up, but Nora really wants to put on some sort of show, so we've agreed to it. She'd be awfully hurt if we hadn't. But you will come, won't you? Can you get away from your work? You could stay at the house for a night or two and not in one of those awful Spellbridge hotels."

I was staring at him. "Did you say *Felix* and I?"

He frowned deeply into his soup, as if, after all, it had not been what he wanted.

"Yes," he said. "I know I ought to have said that first. Felix is going to be the other witness. Do you mind?"

I thought about it for a moment. I have never pretended

that I mind meeting Felix. The truth is, I usually enjoy it if I do not have to see too much of him.

"It isn't an insuperable difficulty," I said. "But if he's going to be there you'll have at least one friend with you."

"Only it would be so nice if you'd come too."

"How did you get hold of him?"

"I asked him over the phone a few days ago. We've always kept in touch, though we don't meet often. But he never mentions you, so I've never been sure if you were a painful subject. But if you aren't, that's fine. I can count on you coming, can't I?"

I nodded. "Yes, if you want me."

So that was how, a week later, Felix and I met again after a rather longer interval than usual. It was at least six months since I had seen him last. I had often thought that it would have been better for us both if we had broken off our connection completely, but he had never seemed to have the same feeling. He had a way of insinuating himself into my life from time to time, sometimes because he had got it into his head, usually mistakenly, that I could help him with some problem that had arisen, sometimes because something had brought him into my neighbourhood and he wanted free lodging for the night, and sometimes, apparently, because he simply felt that he would like a little of my company.

Oddly enough, it was hardly ever to borrow money. He did not mind helping himself from my handbag to pay the bill when he took me out to dinner, but that was a habit that he had got into when we were married and he had never thought that he ought to give it up. He often borrowed from unwary people who certainly never saw their money again, but not from me, though he must have known that I should have found it very difficult to refuse him if he had ever asked me for any, always supposing that I had some to spare myself. My salary did not amount to much and the money that I had inherited from my parents had shrunk with inflation, though the house that they had left me and to which I had returned after Felix and I separated had been a great help. But he seemed to have scruples about asking me directly for money, though he must often have needed it. He had scruples about all kinds of things, but what principle there was behind them had always been a mystery to me. He undoubtedly had a conscience of a kind; I had never been able to fathom how it worked.

After my lunch with Gavin he and I had gone to a jeweller whom he happened to know and Gavin had chosen a necklace for Rosie made of strands of different-coloured gold. I did not really help him to choose it, but when he had decided on it I told him that if anyone had given me such a thing I should have been very happy. There had been a time when Felix gave me lavish presents and I had delighted in them until I found out that he had a way of acquiring them without ever paying for them. He had been, and I was sure still was, an expert shoplifter. The discovery had been one of the first things that brought discord into our marriage. To this day I am not sure how much of my distress was on moral grounds and how much it had been simply that I had been horribly frightened, certain that sooner or later he was bound to be caught. But somehow this had never happened. He was both cautious and very adroit and had never been detected.

At times I had had the sombre thought that it would do him good to be caught, that the shock might cure him, but more often I had simply prayed that he might be cured by some miracle, some profound and shattering experience that would bring about a character change. Unfortunately the miracle had never happened and it was our marriage, suffering from a number of other disquieting things that I had gradually discovered about him, and which I had been much too naïve to understand when I met him first, that had been shattered.

I drove up to Spellbridge on a grey, windless day. It was early November. The trees that I could see from the motorway had turned copper, lightened here and there with the delicate pale gold of birch trees. As the leaves had not yet fallen the scene still had the gentle charm of autumn. I had managed to rearrange my appointments at the clinic where I worked so that I had three clear days ahead of me. The drive to Spellbridge took me about four hours. I had never been there before, but I knew from Gavin that it was a medium-sized industrial town, perhaps less black than it would have been a generation ago, but without any sense of either history or modernity to make it interesting.

The Brownlows did not live in the town itself but in a village about fifteen miles out of it, called Charlwood. That is to say, once upon a time Charlwood had been fifteen miles from the town, but as I drove along the ring road round it, then took the turning that led to the village, I discovered that the suburbs of Spellbridge had almost reached it. Council estates with extensive shopping centres covered what only a few years ago would have been open farmland. Here and there a few groves of trees had been left behind by the developers, but for the most part straight roads and brick and concrete had spread in all directions, giving way, only a mile or two before a sign by the roadside told me that I was entering Charlwood, to hedges and ploughed fields and fields of stubble.

The Brownlows' house had an imposing gateway with a small griffin perched on top of each of the brick gateposts. The house was Georgian, compact and not really very big, but with an air of decorous dignity that made it impressive. It was surrounded by well-kept lawns with a group of beech trees, gloriously russet, near it. I drove up the short drive to the door, got out of my car, took my suitcase off the back seat and rang the bell.

It was answered almost at once by a woman whom I recognized as Hannah Brownlow. She had changed far less than her brother since I had seen her last. Her hair was still black and she still wore it as she had then, drawn straight back from her face and pinned up in a roll at the back of her head. I knew that she was about thirty-five. She was taller than I was, thin, very straight, dressed in jeans and a loose brown sweater. She had her brother's fine-drawn features, but she had a totally different kind of expression on her face. There was no vagueness there, no shy geniality. She looked aloof, rather hard, even a little suspicious.

"Virginia?" she said questioningly, then thrust out a hand in a sudden, jerky gesture. "Come in. Gavin and my father are still at the office, but they'll be back presently. Felix hasn't arrived yet. He's coming by train. It gets in at five forty-three. Gavin's going to meet him."

She had a harsh voice, as jerky as her movements. Her dark eyes looked me over with slightly disapproving curiosity.

"What shall I do with the car?" I asked. "Shall I leave it where it is?"

"Yes. Gavin can put it in the garage when he gets in." Darting forward, she snatched my case from me before I could protest that I could carry it myself. "Let's take this up to your room. Then we'll have some tea. Would you like tea? Or would you sooner have a drink? Perhaps it's early for a drink. I never know what to offer people. I don't usually drink myself, so I don't really know what they'd like. The others will have a drink when they get in."

I said that tea would be nice.

She took me up a graceful, curving staircase to my room. It was square, with a high ceiling, and was handsomely furnished with what I, in my ignorance of such things, took to be pieces that belonged to the same period as the house. Only the bed, covered with a fine patchwork bedspread, had a reassuringly modern look. There were two sash windows overlooking the garden behind the house.

"The bathroom's across there," Hannah said, putting down

my suitcase and pointing at a door facing mine across the passage outside. "Come down when you're ready. I'll get the tea." She left me abruptly.

I opened my case, unpacked the few things that I had brought, combed my hair, then went to one of the windows and looked out.

The scene that I saw had great charm. It was difficult to realize that, only a little way off, the sort of countryside at which I was looking had vanished under the streets and houses through which I had found my way here. The garden itself did not extend very far. A broad path led down the middle of it between herbaceous borders to a walled vegetable garden. There was hardly anything in bloom in the borders but some dahlias and Michaelmas daisies. There was only one house in sight, a low, grey stone building with a slate roof, separated from the Brownlows' by a big meadow and with one or two outbuildings near it.

I wondered if this was where the Flints lived. The land around the house suggested a market garden, with all the plants in it laid out in straight rows. As I watched I saw someone come out of the house, a short, sturdy figure in trousers and an anorak, carrying a spade. I thought it was a woman, though at this distance I could not be sure. Mrs. Flint, perhaps, Rosie's mother. Wondering if I should meet Rosie that day or not until tomorrow at the register office, I turned away from the window and went downstairs to rejoin Hannah.

She was crossing the hall, carrying a tea tray, as I came down the stairs.

"In here," she said and led the way into a spacious drawing room.

It was a beautiful room with a ceiling of delicately moulded plaster, what looked like an Adam fireplace in which a log fire was burning, three windows that reached from floor to ceiling, curtained in velvet of a soft golden colour, some rather stiff-looking armchairs, covered in dark green damask, and some fine rugs on the floor. But something worried me about the room. I did not identify the feeling immediately, but after a few minutes I realized that it was simply that there was nothing wrong with it. There was nothing out of place. Except for the crackling of the fire, there was no sign that the room was ever used. It looked like an exquisitely maintained exhibit in a museum. Not being a particularly tidy person myself, I was a little overpowered.

Hannah poured out the tea from a silver teapot into some green and gold Rockingham cups and offered me a slice of fruitcake. The silver shone and the cake was certainly home-made. I began to wonder about the domestic arrangements of the family. Was Hannah responsible for all this perfection, or had she help? I asked her and she told me that a woman from the village came in to clean every morning, but that was all.

"And I'd get on just as well without her," she said. "You know how it is with people like that. You have to go round after them, putting things straight again. They never learn the right places for things. Don't you agree?"

My feeling on that matter was that I did not mind what they did, so long as I did not have to do it myself.

She went on, "As I remember it, Felix used to do a good deal of your cooking. He was a good cook, I believe."

"Excellent," I said. "It's been one of the things I've really missed since we separated."

"I'm a good cook," she said. "I take a great interest in it."

It is an odd thing I have often noticed that people who would never claim to be talented at anything else, even when they really are, do not hesitate to tell you that they are good cooks.

"That must be nice for your family," I said. "Can Rosie cook?"

She gave a short laugh with a touch of scorn in it. "I expect she can scramble an egg. She's got a job in Spellbridge and I imagine thinks mere domestic things are beneath her. But

Gavin won't notice. I can take all the trouble in the world over a meal and it doesn't seem to mean anything to him. Sometimes I think he doesn't even know what he's eaten. It's very discouraging. But luckily my father's quite different. He always appreciates what I do for him. You've never met him, have you?"

"No."

"You'll find he's a wonderful person. He's got tremendous charm and he's considerate and understanding, too, not like most men. But perhaps you'll think he's old-fashioned. He's quite worried, you know, about having you and Felix here at the same time. That's the sort of thing he doesn't understand. Not that he'll show it. He's far too courteous."

"If it's going to worry him, one of us could go to a hotel," I said.

"Oh no, not now that it's all arranged. He never likes it if one changes one's plans, once they're made. That's one of the reasons he and Gavin don't get on better than they do. You never know where you are with Gavin. He's always springing things on you without warning."

"Gavin told me that they get on pretty well now," I said.

"That's the kind of thing he would say," she said disparagingly. "He doesn't want to face how much of a strain it's been for Father, putting up with his casual ways. And he's only come back to live here because it happens to be convenient for him, now that he's working in the office in Spellbridge. Of course, it's his home and naturally Father made him welcome, but personally I don't much care for simply being made use of. Gavin's never cared for anybody but Gavin. Look how he treated Kay."

I did not know much about how Gavin had treated Kay. I only knew that Kay, who was a beautiful but very egocentric young woman, had swept swiftly through a series of love affairs both before and after her marriage and that Gavin had found that it was more than he could endure. She had admitted this to me herself. For some reason, although she and I were so different, we had always got on rather well. But it had not surprised me that the marriage had not lasted long and I had never thought of Gavin as to blame for its breakdown.

"But I suppose he cares a good deal for Rosie, doesn't he?" I said.

Hannah gave another of her abrupt laughs. "I'll tell you what he cares about, that's Rosie's money. Not that it's Rosie's, it's her mother's, but Nora Flint will give Rosie anything she wants and Rosie doesn't mind asking. She's quite a greedy child, in my opinion."

I thought of the sturdy figure, carrying a spade, whom I had seen from my bedroom window.

"I hadn't realized the Flints were wealthy," I said.

"They weren't, until a few months ago. They just had their market garden, a quite small one, which only brought in a bare living. They employ only one man and Nora does all the rest of the work without much help from Oliver. But then Nora suddenly inherited a lot of money from some grandaunt or other. It happened about last Easter, I think. I don't know how much it is, but I know they're relatively rich now. And Gavin suddenly got interested in Rosie, whom he'd hardly noticed before."

"Somehow I can't see Gavin being so very interested in money," I said. "He never seemed to worry about it much in the old days."

She gave a sardonic smile, contemptuous of my simplicity.

Looking at her, thinking that she had been meant to be a beautiful woman, with her finely modelled features, her big, dark eyes with their long, shadowy fringes of lashes and her small, well-shaped head, I wondered what had soured her so deeply, particularly in her relationship with her brother. I know that the real life of any family is always a puzzling, secret thing and that hatred and jealousy can be under the surface, sometimes all mixed up with genuine love, but Hannah was making no secret of her feelings for Gavin. I hoped that he would arrive soon with Felix, because I was beginning to take a dislike to her and I always find the feeling of disliking another person, whether I feel I can show it or not, a disagreeable strain.

But it was her father who arrived first.

I had a vague picture of him in my mind by then, made up of the things that Hannah had just said about him, together with the odds and ends that I remembered Gavin having said. Hannah had said that he was considerate and understanding, appreciative of her cooking and all that she did for him, old-fashioned and perhaps a bit rigid and out of tune with his son, yet making him welcome in his old home when he had wanted to return to it. Gavin had spoken of him as a shrewd businessman who had been successful in his profession although he had little real talent, a possessive man, domineering, prejudiced. So what I was expecting was someone dignified and courteous, but perhaps stiff and unapproachable, a tall man, probably, with the good looks of both his children.

I was quite wrong. Gavin's and Hannah's good looks must have come from their long-dead mother, for Edward Brownlow was almost an ugly man. He had a curiously crumpled-looking face in which small grey eyes, a short nose with flaring nostrils and a small, down-curving mouth were set in a mask of wrinkles. His hair was grey and there was not much of it left. He was a small man, but he held himself very erect, as if to make the most of his height. He was dressed in a double-breasted dark blue suit which was old-fashioned in cut but certainly expensive. At first glance I thought that there was an air of petulance about him, but that was before he had caught sight of me and come quickly towards me with his hand out and an attractive smile on his face.

"Mrs. Freer," he said. "I'm so sorry I wasn't here to greet you when you arrived, but I see Hannah's been looking after you."

"We call her Virginia," Hannah said. "She's an old friend of Gavin's, in case you'd forgotten."

"Virginia? Yes, of course. You came by car, I believe, Virginia. Did you have a pleasant drive?"

"How could she?" Hannah said. "No driving's pleasant nowadays."

"How true," he said. "Alas for the old days, when it was possible to enjoy it. Alas for the old days for all sorts of reasons. You're too young to remember, but this country was so very beautiful once. Even a few miles from a dreary little Victorian slum like Spellbridge, the country was a delight. And where is it now? Gone forever. Nothing will ever bring it back. I suppose your husband—that's to say, Mr. Freer—Felix, that's his name, isn't it? My memory for names is terrible. I suppose he hasn't arrived yet."

"He and Gavin should be here any time now," Hannah said.

She always broke in quickly before I could answer, almost as if she were jealous of any contact anyone but herself might make with her father.

"I suppose that tea's cold," he went on. "I shouldn't mind a cup of tea."

She stood up at once. "I'll make some more."

"No, no, don't trouble," he said. "Please don't trouble. I'll have a drink when the others get in." He sat down on one of the stiff, damask-covered chairs and Hannah sat down again on hers. "You aren't smoking, Virginia. I'm sorry I can't offer you a cigarette, but none of us smokes in this house. Hannah would never allow it. Hannah rules us, you know, benevolently, of course, but with a rod of iron. We all do what we're told."

I do not smoke myself, but Felix is an incurable chain smoker. I wondered how he would manage when he got here.

Edward Brownlow continued, "It's so good of you to come to our little celebration tomorrow. I shan't be present myself. Gavin made it plain that he didn't expect it of me, which suits me very well. Weddings and funerals both depress me. They raise so many unanswerable questions about the future. We'll all meet later at the reception the Flints insist on giving. There'll be champagne, I suppose, which I dislike, and a speech or two, which I shall dislike even more. Flint will undoubtedly want to make one. He never misses the chances of talking when he's got a captive audience. And Gavin may have to say a few appropriate words, which he'll stutter over very incompetently. Luckily the groom's father isn't expected to say anything, in fact he's about the most unimportant person present on an occasion like this. I've wondered if it would be noticed if I didn't appear at all, but Hannah tells me I must and Hannah always knows what's right—don't you, my dear?" He reached out and laid a hand on her shoulder. "I don't know where I'd be without her to keep me on the rails."

There was something mawkish in his tone which embarrassed me, but Hannah could not have felt it, for she smiled at him with the nearest thing to sweetness that I had yet seen on her hard, handsome face.

"Well, you don't want to offend the Flints, now that they've got money," she said. "It wouldn't be fair to Gavin."

He gave a shake of his head. "There you go again, harping on Gavin marrying Rosie for her money. You really shouldn't, my dear. But I agree with you it's difficult to understand his enthusiasm for a girl like Rosie after living with someone like Kay. She and I always got on splendidly. I never believed the stories I was told about her. I know she was very attractive to men, but that was hardly her fault. Rosie, I'm afraid, dislikes me. Not that she's uncivil, but one can always tell. . . . Oh, here they are, Gavin and your husband."

He got to his feet as footsteps sounded in the hall and the door opened.

"Come in, come in," he said genially and held out his hand to Felix, who preceded Gavin into the room.

CHAPTER 2

I was always taken by surprise, when I saw Felix, at the way that he had managed to acquire an air of quiet distinction. Boyish charm had lasted him well into his thirties, but he had abandoned this some time ago in favour of a look of dignity and reserve which would have suited a successful consultant in Harley Street or a leading executive in some important industry.

In fact, when I had seen him last, he was working for a seedy firm of private detectives, and before that he had been a salesman in a very shady firm of secondhand car dealers, whom he had left only when he had begun to feel that they were breaking the law too dangerously often even for him. When we had got married I had believed that he was a civil engineer, working for a big firm of contractors, but in the end I had stumbled on the fact that this was only one of his fantasies and that they had never even heard of him.

I had never managed to make up my mind how much he himself believed in his fantasies while they lasted, but they had driven me fairly desperate while I was living with him and I think it was that particular discovery that had made me decide that I could not stand it any longer. It had put an end to my hope that somehow, if only my love for him could survive, I might be able to cure him and induce him to live in the real world. But I suppose the truth was that my love had already died a quiet death, though a kind of affection had always lingered on, and when I had made up my mind to leave him, sad though it had seemed in some ways, it had felt wonderfully peaceful to live alone, with my feet on solid ground, instead of never being able to feel sure when I should find myself bogged down in the quagmire of his imagination.

Today he was wearing a grey suit which looked both good and new, so it seemed unlikely that he was still working for the firm of private detectives, who had not paid him lavishly. His good looks were wearing well. His age was forty-one, the same as mine, but he did not look it, although there were threads of grey in his fair hair. He was a slender man of medium height, with a triangular face, wide at the temples, pointed at the chin, with curiously drooping eyelids that made his vivid blue eyes look almost triangular too. His mouth was wide and friendly. The friendliness was one of the most genuine things about him, for he liked almost everybody, just so long as they did not go out of their way to show that they had taken a dislike to him. If that happened he could retaliate with vicious swiftness, but on the whole he was as tolerant of everyone as he wanted them to be of him and could mix happily with the most extraordinarily dissimilar types of people.

After he had shaken hands with Edward Brownlow and with Hannah, he came over to me and kissed me on the cheek.

"Gavin told me you'd be here," he said. "It's nice to see you."

I said that it was nice to see him. That, after six years of separation, just about described our relationship. Hannah removed the tea tray and Gavin brought out drinks. Hannah did not return. I guessed that she was busy in the kitchen, preparing dinner, and suggested that I might go to help her, but her father said that Hannah never welcomed help.

"She's used to handling things by herself and says that if anyone tries to help her they only get in her way," he said. "She's very independent. Now will you excuse me? There's a little work I'd like to attend to before dinner. Gavin, Felix would like to unpack, I expect. You can show him his room. We've given our best spare room to Virginia, Felix, but I hope you'll be comfortable. And have another drink first."

Very erect, with the look of trying to make himself taller than he was, Edward Brownlow walked out of the room. Gavin started to pour out a second round of drinks for us, but Felix quickly covered his glass with his hand. He was a very cautious drinker, always afraid, I thought, that only a little alcohol might make him lose his grip on the part that he happened to be playing.

. "No, thanks," he said. "That drink you gave me on the way here was quite enough for me."

Gavin explained to me that they had stopped for a drink on the way from the station.

"I wanted to tell Felix a little about the situation here," he said. "I hadn't told him you were coming. And there's Hannah too—I mean, the mood she's in. You may have noticed it. She's being even more awkward than usual, and that's saying a good deal. The trouble is, I think, she seemed to be on the edge of getting engaged to a friend of ours, Paul Haycock. My father was very keen about it. Paul's quite an important man locally. He's a partner in a big firm of chartered accountants and he's on the town council. Then suddenly the whole thing was off. We don't know exactly why, because you don't ask Hannah about that sort of thing, but she stopped going out with him and was obviously very unhappy—except that I think she rather revels in her unhappiness, if you know what I mean. I'm sure the best thing is to take as little notice of how she acts up as possible."

I doubted if that was really the best recipe for dealing with Hannah. I thought that probably people had been taking too little notice of her all her life. But it would certainly be the easiest thing to do.

Sipping my drink while Gavin took Felix up to his bedroom, I lingered on in the empty room, enjoying the bright fire. Then, as I put down my empty glass, I thought suddenly that I should like to go up to my own room and change out of the suit that I had been wearing all day into a dress, even though I did not think it was likely that Hannah would change for dinner out of her jeans and sweater. So I went upstairs, took off my suit and hung it in the wardrobe, had a wash, put on a new dress that I had brought with me of red and grey printed jersey, and had reached the stage of putting on fresh make-up when there was a tap on the door and Felix came into the room.

He lit a cigarette and sat down on the edge of the bed.

"Well, how are things with you?" he asked.

"Quite satisfactory," I answered. "And you're looking very prosperous. Are you still working for those private detectives?"

"No, not for some time now," he said. "The job was just too sordid and the pay was negligible. I'm working for a firm of house agents and looking prosperous is part of the job. It's quite interesting work. I like it. You meet all kinds of people and, as you know, I'm quite a good salesman. But when you're trying to persuade someone to spend a hundred to two hundred thousand on a house, you don't want to look as if to yourself sums like that are the stuff of which dreams are made. When you see someone edging up to convincing himself that he can afford that dear little place that his wife's fallen in love with, all beams and thatch and inconvenience, on which they're going to have to spend another twenty thousand to make it habitable, it's important to look as if you're taking it all as a matter of course. The trouble is, I get more excited than I should. The thought of large sums of money, even if they aren't mine, always has that effect on me."

"It sounds to me as if, for you, it's almost an honest job," I said.

"Up to a point," he said. He strolled across the room and dropped some ash from his cigarette into a pretty little Chel-

sea bowl on the mantelpiece. "One's under no actual obliga-
tion to point out the dry rot, or the damp, or that they're
going to build a motorway right past the door in a year or
two, or mention the fact that a murder was once committed
there. It's up to the client to find out that sort of thing for
himself. But it always upsets me a little to waste most of
someone's day by taking them to look at something which I
know is going to turn out utterly unsuitable—though, as a
matter of fact, that's something it's hard to be sure of. People
are so extraordinary. They often end up buying the opposite
of what they asked for in the first place."

"Tell me, have you ever knowingly sold a house where a
murder had been committed?" I asked.

"Well . . ." He hesitated and I thought that he was about
to tell me some gruesome story which he was making up as he
went along, but either the inspiration for one did not come or
else he was in one of his more truthful moods. "Not actually,
no, though you sometimes get the feeling in a house that
awful things must have happened there. But naturally, if the
client doesn't seem to have the same sort of feeling, and some
people are very insensitive, you don't mention it to him. You
know, I think this house has a peculiar atmosphere. I don't
feel really happy in it. Do you?"

"It's too clean and tidy for me," I admitted. "I like a bit of
mess around the place."

"I don't mean that. It's what I said, the atmosphere . . ."

"I should say it's just that the people in it are rather at
odds with one another."

"Perhaps that's it. For Gavin's sake, it's a good thing he's
getting out of it. He told me he and Rosie have taken a flat in
Spellbridge. I'm looking forward to seeing what Rosie's like.
Will she be the opposite of Kay, or is Gavin one of the people who are doomed to make the same mistake over and over
again? Not that I find it easy to think of Kay as a mistake.
Did I ever tell you . . . ?" He paused again.

I put some lipstick on my mouth and said, "Did you tell me what?"

"I was wondering if I'd ever told you that I once thought I was in love with her," he said.

"Would that have been before or after we separated?" I asked.

"It was before I'd even met you. We were both very young and she was just about the loveliest thing I'd ever seen. I came quite near to asking her to marry me."

"Would she have accepted you?"

"I don't think so. I don't think she was in a marrying mood yet."

"Were you lovers?"

"Not even that. No, it was just a daydream I had for a little while."

I did not doubt that he was telling me the truth. Sexually Felix was not secretive, though he was not boastful either. The stories he told me that I mistrusted most concerned professional successes, money that he had acquired and improbable acts of heroism.

"Perhaps it's a pity you didn't marry her," I said. "She might have suited you much better than I did. Do you ever see her now?"

"Occasionally. It seems to me she's even more beautiful than she was when she was young."

"If you feel like that, why don't you try taking things up where you left off?"

He shook his head with a touch of sadness. "I think there's someone else on the scene. The last time we met she talked rather sentimentally about the advantages of marriage and positively blushed when I asked her if she was thinking about it for herself. Can you imagine Kay blushing? But I swear she did. Of course she said she hadn't meant it like that, but I didn't quite believe her. And there's the minor impediment from my point of view that I'm still married to you."

"That could be remedied."

"Divorce, you mean? You're always talking about divorce. Don't you hate the idea of letting a lot of complete strangers paw over your private affairs, and then paying them a lot for doing it? I think there's something very distasteful about it."

"But it would at least tidy things up between us and might be a good thing in the end."

"I thought you didn't like things to be too clean and tidy."

"I was talking about this house, which is quite a different thing. It's unnaturally overorganized. I think Hannah must be obsessively domesticated."

"You aren't thinking of getting married again yourself, are you?" he said. "If you are, of course I shouldn't stand in your way."

"No, that hasn't arisen. By the way, have you still got the flat in Little Carbery Street?"

"Oh yes, I shan't give that up unless I go really broke, though I know something about its value now. Properties in that part of London have gone up enormously since we bought it. I could get at least forty thousand for it and there are times when forty thousand seems very attractive."

Irrationally, I was glad that he had not parted with the flat where we had spent the three years of our marriage, which had begun with more happiness than I had ever known before or since and ended in such desperation that I had once seriously considered swallowing a bottleful of barbiturates as the simplest way out of an intolerable situation. Going to the flat, as I still occasionally did, was always extremely painful to me, and yet I found something consoling in the thought that it was there, that something out of that short period in my life had lasted.

I had finished with my make-up.

"We'd better be going down," I said.

Felix stubbed out his cigarette in the Chelsea bowl and we went downstairs together.

I had been wrong to think that Hannah would not change out of her jeans and sweater. We found her in the drawing room, wearing a severe yet elegant dress of dark brown velvet and a pair of long gold earrings. She looked formidable but astonishingly handsome. Gavin was there too, nursing another drink. Their father joined us and we all went into the dining room, which was very like the drawing room in its dimensions and its furnishing, though its dominant colour was a somewhat overpowering red which made me think of underdone steak as the most appropriate thing to eat there. But our first course consisted of a very delicate cucumber and cream cheese mousse, followed by pork chops cooked in cider and then a black currant sorbet. Hannah had not exaggerated when she said that she was a good cook.

But unfortunately she was not a good hostess. She sat mute and obscurely hostile to us all at one end of the long table while her father talked. It was mainly about a new project in which his firm was involved, the designing of a building estate which, as far as I could make out, would bring Spellbridge even closer to Charlwood than it was already. Because of this, I found his enthusiasm for the scheme surprising, and supposed that the fact that there was a great deal of money in it must outweigh everything else. But then he explained that the new buildings would not be visible from this house and so would not damage its amenity. Furthermore, the blocks of flats that were to be erected would not be council houses but would be something quite special.

However, I felt that Gavin did not share his father's feelings about the scheme, for he sat looking abstracted and was almost as silent as Hannah, which might have been, of course, merely because he was dreaming about Rosie and his marriage tomorrow, but in its way it was disconcerting. It was only Felix, with his new professional concern with property and its prices, who responded with any interest to Edward Brownlow's steady monologue.

Knowing that he did not intend to be present at Gavin's wedding next day, I supposed that the architect would be going as usual to his office, but when I came down to breakfast that morning I found him in his dressing gown, swallowing aspirins with his coffee.

"It's a pity, I'm not too well," he said. His voice was hoarse, as if his throat were sore. "I think I may be developing flu. I hope I don't pass it on to any of you. One of our chaps in the office was complaining about it a day or two ago. I told him he ought to have stayed at home. Being heroic about it and coming to work wasn't really considerate to anybody. Of course at this time of year there's always a lot of it about."

"All you want is an excuse not to have to go to the reception this afternoon," Hannah said severely.

Wearing her jeans and sweater again, she was in her place at the head of the table with Felix on her right. He had finished his breakfast and was looking fidgety, because he wanted a cigarette but felt that it might cause friction if he lit one. Gavin appeared to have finished his breakfast too and gone out. As I sat down at the table Felix gave a thoughtful look out of the window, considering going into the garden for his smoke, but a fine rain was falling, hardly more than a mist, though enough to discourage any idea of strolling about out of doors. The day was the peculiarly gloomy kind, without being really cold, that comes so often in November, with a leaden sky and enough wind to send beech leaves fluttering past the window. A few more days like this and the trees would be bare.

"Oh, I'll go to the reception, even if it means handing on the plague to everyone else in the room," Edward Brownlow said. "You've convinced me it would be grossly discourteous not to go, and an excuse like flu, even when it's perfectly genuine, never sounds convincing. I must go and do a good job of admiring the wedding presents and waving good-bye to the happy pair when they set off. But then I can come home, have some brandy to take the taste of the champagne out of my mouth and go to bed. The thought of that will keep me going."

"I've promised Nora I'll go round early and help with arranging the presents and putting out the glasses and so on," Hannah said. "I'll go straight after lunch."

"You won't see my present there," Edward Brownlow said with a smile. "I've given them a cheque, which is the one kind of present one can feel certain will be appreciated, but it can hardly be put on exhibition."

My own present to Rosie and Gavin was an old fruit bowl of Waterford glass, which I had found in an antique shop near my home. I wondered what Felix had given them and whether he had paid for it, or had slipped it quietly into his pocket while the shop assistant who had been attending to something that he was buying legitimately had been looking another way. In any case, it would probably be something attractive. Felix really enjoyed giving presents, all the more, however, when he had not had to pay for them, which was not at all from meanness but was more because he felt that it was a trophy of the chase, a kind of triumph.

I asked him about this later when Hannah had left us to do some shopping in the village, making it plain that she did not require our company, and her father had returned to his room to dress, and the woman from the village had arrived, had cleared the breakfast table and gone about her work.

"What did I give them?" he said. We were in the drawing room where he had given up trying to resist his desire for a cigarette and in the absence of ashtrays was dropping the ash into the grate, where a fresh fire had been laid but not yet lit. "I gave them a food blender."

This was so unlike him that I said automatically, "I don't believe it."

"Yes, I simply couldn't think of anything else," he said. "I thought half a dozen other people were sure to give them food blenders, so they'll be able to return them to the shops they came from without offending anybody, and either get the money back or choose something they really want. It was an indirect way of sending a cheque, which I hadn't the nerve to do. For one thing, I couldn't think of the sort of amount that would look right, coming from someone like me. Anything I could actually afford somehow looked mean."

I thought that at least a food blender was not something that you could slip into your pocket without being noticed, so Gavin and Rosie were not in receipt of stolen property. Gavin joined us a few minutes later, saying that he had been packing. He looked keyed up and excited.

"We're going to Cornwall," he said. "It seemed as good a place to go to as any at this time of year. At least it'll be quiet. We couldn't stand the idea of the crowds on the Canaries, or in the Caribbean, or anywhere like that. Are you ready to go? We ought to be leaving soon. We're going to pick up Rosie, then drive on into Spellbridge."

I was wearing the suit in which I had arrived the day before, but in view of the rain I thought that I should take a coat to wear over it. I said that I could be ready in a minute and went up to my room to fetch the coat. When I came down again I found Edward Brownlow, dressed now, in the drawing room.

He had a hand on Gavin's shoulder and was saying, "You know I don't mean half the things I say, Gavin. I wish you and Rosie very well. She's a nice child, a sweet child, and I sincerely hope you'll be very happy together. And I know Hannah feels the same, even if she doesn't know how to say it. We're both delighted to welcome Rosie into the family."

I did not believe that he meant a word of it. Gavin started to mumble something in reply but broke off as the telephone in the hall began to ring.

Hannah answered it. She had just returned from her shopping and was crossing the hall when the ringing started. I heard her speaking, then she came into the room and said to her father, "It's for you. It's Stephen."

Edward Brownlow frowned. "Stephen? Now what does *he* want?"

He went out of the room.

Gavin explained, "Stephen Ledbetter. He's our solicitor. He doesn't usually ring up here, but I suppose he tried the office first and was told that Father hadn't come in."

Whatever the call was about, it seemed to disturb Edward Brownlow. As Gavin, Felix and I were crossing the hall to leave the house, he was saying angrily, "Haycock? . . . It isn't possible. . . . All right, all right, just as you say!"

He slammed the telephone down, standing looking after us as Gavin opened the front door and made way for Felix and me to go out ahead of him. The old man's small grey eyes had a glazed look of dismay in them. It was almost as if he did not see us. Then, just before Gavin pulled the door shut after us, his father caught hold of it and held it open.

"Gavin, I may change my mind and not go to the reception after all," he said. "You won't mind, will you? The truth is, I don't feel as well as I thought I did."

A flush on his cheekbones showed up harshly on his withered cheeks. He did not look at all well.

"That's all right," Gavin said, though he looked put out. "I know it isn't the kind of thing you care for."

Edward Brownlow passed a hand across his forehead. "That isn't it at all. I didn't mean to let you down. But my head's getting worse and I've got the shivers. I'm sorry about it—very—but I'm sure you understand."

"Better get Dr. Black," Gavin said. "He'll give you something for it."

"No, I'll stick to aspirins and go to bed. Good luck to you now and my blessing, if you think that will do any good, coming from an old sinner like me."

He smiled at Gavin, then closed the door after him.

The three of us walked towards the garage through the thin, cold rain. Gavin was frowning when we got into the car and looked most unsuitably depressed for the occasion, but neither Felix nor I tried to say anything encouraging. There was something in the situation that I did not understand. It was obvious that the sudden worsening in Edward Brownlow's health was the result of the telephone call that he had just received from his solicitor, and that Gavin not only thought so too but had guessed what the call had been about. He stayed sombre-looking until we had turned off the road into the narrow, rutted drive that led to the Flints' house, then he seemed to come to himself, though it appeared to be an effort to shake off whatever had been weighing on his mind.

The house was the one that I had seen from my bedroom window. It was a low, stone cottage which might have been built in the seventeenth century. But there is something ageless about stone houses. The stone itself is so immeasurably old that nothing built in it can look recent. However, the small windows and the low doorway and a look the house had of having been quarried out of the ground it stood on made me certain that it had stood there for some hundreds of years.

It was surrounded by well-cultivated patches of leeks and brussels sprouts and cabbages. Gavin stopped the car in front of it and honked his horn twice. Immediately the door was thrown open and a girl came running out. Scrambling into the front seat, which Felix and I had left empty for her, she threw her arms round Gavin's neck and kissed him ecstatically. Then she twisted round in her seat and held out her hand to me and to Felix.

"I'm so glad you came," she said. "It really wouldn't have felt like getting married at all if we'd just had to sweep two strangers in off the street to witness our signatures. Not that my parents wouldn't have come, but as Gavin's family didn't seem keen on it, we thought it would look a bit as if mine were trying to take possession of us. And you're such very old friends of his, it's marvellous to have you here."

There was a wonderful glow about her. She was a very pretty girl who looked even younger than her twenty-three years. She had thick, straight golden hair, cut in a fringe across her forehead and falling richly to her shoulders, light brown eyes with a golden glint in them and creamy skin, just touched with rose on her cheekbones. But besides the beauty that nature had given her, there was a charming liveliness and good nature in her face. She was of medium height and slender and was wearing the necklace that I had helped Gavin to choose for her, with a white silk blouse and a suit of green and white tweed which looked so new that I was sure it had been bought specially for this occasion. She had a white rose pinned to her lapel. In fact, I thought, she had done her best to look bridal and would really have been happiest, if Gavin's divorce had not prevented it, to wear lace and orange blossom and to walk up the aisle of the village church on her father's arm.

But if she could not have exactly what she wanted, she was not going to let it dampen her high spirits. As Gavin turned the car she spoke over her shoulder to Felix and me. "Poor Gavin's looking terrible, isn't he? Men always feel terrible at a time like this, so one's been told. Did you feel terrible when you got married, Felix?"

"Well, naturally, but who wouldn't, marrying Virginia?" he said. "And how right I turned out to be."

"Because of your separating later, you mean." She said it casually, accepting our disjointed relationship without any fuss, which was a relief, because both of us dislike having to explain it. "I wonder if Gavin and I will ever separate. It seems too unspeakably awful to be thinking about that just now, and yet, d'you know, I find it terribly difficult to convince myself that a few things one says, just in a few minutes, and then signing one's name, can actually affect the way you're going to spend the whole of the rest of your life." She turned to Gavin. "It *will* all be over in a few minutes, won't it?"

"Only a few," he answered.

"Of course, he's experienced," she went on, "as he's been through it all before. And I know he's going to hate going through it again, yet when I suggested that in the circumstances nowadays there wasn't much point in bothering about the thing at all, he was quite upset. Anyway, the only way to get him was to agree to marry him, even if it has to be at a dreary old registrar's."

Yes, I thought, she would really have liked a church and organ music and her father in a morning coat, even if it came from Moss Bros., and her mother in a new hat and silk two-piece. And I wondered if the reception in the afternoon was genuinely because her mother wanted it or because her mother had realized how much Rosie wanted it herself.

Driving through the council estates and the more solid suburbs of the town, we entered Spellbridge. It must once have been a prosperous town, to judge by the pretentiousness of its main street, but it had depended on steel and was said to be in a bad way nowadays. There was certainly an air of gloom about it, though perhaps that came more from the dreary wetness of the day and the depressing architecture than from anything else. I doubted if there was a single thing worth looking at in the town. Most of it had been built about the middle of the nineteenth century and where the grime of the last hundred years had been cleaned away, as it had been here and there, brickwork of the sullen red that never weathers had been revealed. It was pompous but undistinguished and might just as well have been left concealed by soot.

The Town Hall was an enormous building, mock Gothic in style, which must have been built at a time when the city fathers had optimistically assumed that Spellbridge would one day amount to something, instead of sliding downhill into obscurity. We could find no parking place close to the register office, so we had to leave the car some distance away and walk through the rain. Rosie had not been as prudent as I had and brought a coat and by the time that we reached the entrance to the office her bright hair was spangled with raindrops and there was a sheen of moisture on her pretty suit.

As we went in we met another couple coming out. They were both extremely young, neither of them more than nineteen, and the voluminous coat of royal blue that the girl was wearing did not conceal the fact that she was pregnant. The boy had long, wispy hair and wore very tight trousers, a gaudily patterned shirt and a black leather jacket. They were followed by a small, middle-aged couple, both dressed all in grey and with grey, bewildered faces. Probably they were the parents of one of the couple and had been the witnesses at their wedding. Going in as they came out, I had the feeling of being on a kind of conveyor belt and was sure that as we came out we should meet the next couple coming in, which did not help to make this seem a special occasion.

However, the registrar turned out to be a gentle, elderly man with kind eyes and a soft deep voice that made the colourless words of the ceremony sound memorable, and when it was over he shook Rosie and Gavin by the hand and wished them happiness and managed to sound as if he cared about it. He would no doubt be repeating the act all day, but it was pleasant that he was a man who so obviously loved his work.

As we emerged into the street Rosie gave a sudden excited whoop and went running to the car, scrambling into it to get out of the rain. The rest of us plodded after her a good deal more slowly. There was no doubt about it, she was much younger than any of us.

Sounding diffident about it as we got into the car, Gavin

said, "I've booked a table at the Golden Fleece. I hope you'll
like it. It's the only place in Spellbridge where you can get a
decent meal."

"I want a wonderful meal, an enormous meal!" Rosie cried.
"Getting married makes one hungry, isn't that a funny
thing?"

Gavin drove us to the Golden Fleece, which was only a little way further along the main street and was a large, un-
promising-looking, square building, which had a sort of court-
yard at the back where we could park the car and so dive
straight indoors without getting wet again.

Inside the restaurant was far more agreeable than it had appeared from outside. The Victorianism of it, which had obviously been carefully preserved, or perhaps even recreated, by
someone who knew what he was about, had a cosy, welcom-
ing air. Besides the radiators which kept it warm, a big fire
blazed in the fantastically ornate marble fireplace and light
from massive crystal chandeliers dispelled the gloom of the
day. Gavin, who seemed determined to take charge of things
for once, advised us to stick to the roast beef and Yorkshire
pudding, which he said would be very good, but that anything
with a French name was unreliable. We all ordered roast beef
and he ordered some Montrachet to go with it. Felix and I
drank his health and Rosie's, then Felix caught my eye and
almost imperceptibly, with a faintly mocking smile, raised his
glass to me. I smiled blandly back. I did not mean to be
trapped just then into either painful or sentimental memories.

I am not sure when I first noticed that there was something
wrong with the meal. The roast beef was excellent. So was the
wine. Yet a curious silence settled upon us. Almost as soon as
I had become aware of it, I realized that Gavin was its source.
His answers to what was said to him were monosyllabic and
he had nothing to offer himself. He did not quite frown, yet
there was a look of strain on his vague, attractive face. Rosie
did not seem affected by it at first and cheerfully chattered

on, but by degrees her gaiety began to falter; she started to act
as if her only interest in the meal was the food on her plate
and was careful not to let Felix or me meet her eyes, in case
we should see the anxiety in them. But from time to time she
flashed a look of pained entreaty at Gavin, imploring him not
to spoil this day for her, at which he seemed briefly to make
an effort to respond, only to relapse after a moment into silence.

It was then that Felix showed the best side of his nature.
He had perceived as much as I had but, unlike me, was
prepared to do something about it. Finishing his roast beef,
he began to tell a rambling story about something that had
happened to him some years ago in Australia, when he had
been a civil engineer, working on an irrigation project in the
outback. Somehow, he said, he had been separated from his
party deep in the desert and would have died of thirst if he
had not been rescued by a wandering aboriginal tribe. They
had stolen all his clothes and he had had to go stark naked for
some weeks, but they had fed him, though they had made
him work very hard for the food they gave him. He said that
he would not tell us what that food had been, because it
might put us off our roast beef, but at least he had survived
and in the end, taking terrible risks, he had managed to es-
cape to civilization.

Of course, there was not a word of truth in it. He had
never been in Australia in his life and, as I knew only too
well, had never been a civil engineer. He had probably taken
the whole story from some book that he had read recently.
Not that he read very much, except for the financial pages
and the sports pages of various newspapers, but when he
did open a book it was usually an adventure story and he
identified himself so completely with the hero that afterwards
he could repeat it all, as he was doing now, as if it had been
an experience of his own. I am not sure if Rosie believed him,
but she played Desdemona nicely to his Othello and pitied

him charmingly, and though Gavin certainly did not swallow
the story, he seemed grateful that the silence that had de-
scended upon us had been broken.

As Felix brought his tale to an end with a description of
how inhibiting it had felt at first to be compelled to wear
clothes again, Gavin said, "Apple pie and Devonshire cream—
we mustn't miss that, even if it means we're going to be late
for the reception."

Because he sounded normally cheerful once more, Rosie
beamed at him, and I thought what a fool he would be to dis-
appoint this lovely girl, when she so ardently believed in happiness, simply because of some mysterious telephone call that
his father had had from his solicitor.

CHAPTER 3

We were not very late for the reception, though most of the guests had arrived by the time that we reached the Flints' house. As soon as Gavin stopped the car in front of it Rosie's parents came out to greet us. I had been right that the woman with the spade whom I had seen from my bedroom window had been Nora Flint. She was a short, solidly built woman of about forty-five with a square, strong yet ingenuous face that had the ruddiness that came from a life lived mainly out of doors, short, curly brown hair and slightly prominent eyes that looked very blue against her tanned skin. She was wearing a sober navy-blue dress that did not fit her very well, flat-heeled black shoes and no make-up. Kissing Rosie and Gavin, she shook hands with Felix and me, then took Rosie and Gavin each by an arm and led them indoors, leaving her husband to look after us.

Oliver Flint looked a little older than his wife, but he was the sort of man whose appearance changes very little between thirty and sixty. He would always have the same spare figure, the wide, slightly stooping shoulders, the easy, loose-limbed way of moving. He was tall, with slender hips and long legs. His hair was of almost the same colour as Rosie's, though a little darker, and he had her golden-brown eyes. There were a few deep lines on his narrow face, lines of tension rather than age, I thought, but he was a very good-looking man. He took Felix and me into the house, took my coat from me and ushered us into the room where the guests were assembled, warning us as we went in not to bump our heads in the door-way.

It was very low and the room inside had a very low ceiling, ribbed with dark beams. A big log smouldered in an ancient fireplace and there were two small windows set in walls a yard thick. But the furniture was modern, angular and pale, and the pictures, of which there were a great many on the walls, were all photographs, most of them of flowers, though there were some portraits too, a number of them of Rosie at different ages, and a few of Nora. I remembered that Gavin had told me that Oliver Flint was a skilled photographer. Gavin had also said that, although he was an interesting chap, nothing that he had done had ever quite come off. The con-genital amateur, I thought, was what Gavin meant.

Oliver Flint brought Felix and me champagne and intro-duced us to several of the people there. I am always incapable of catching the name of anyone to whom I am introduced and beyond the fact that most of them were neighbours from the village of Charlwood, with a sprinkling of people from Spellbridge and some relatives of the Flints, who had come from some distance, I never took in who they were. Hannah Brownlow was there, in the brown velvet that she had worn the evening before and holding a glass of champagne which she was regarding with an air of deep concentration, as if she were wondering what it might do to her if she did not treat it with great care. I thought that she was probably trying to think of some tactful way of disposing of it without being no-ticed. Edward Brownlow was not there.

I had just been talking to a woman who, I gathered, was the wife of one of the local doctors when I found Oliver Flint at my elbow.

"You and your husband are staying with the Brownlows, aren't you?" he said.

"Yes," I answered, "for a couple of nights."

"They're old friends of yours, I believe."

"Pretty old."

"Your husband's just been telling me that he and Gavin were at school together."

"Ah yes," I said, because that might mean anything.

The truth of the matter was that I knew very little for certain about Felix's education. He usually claimed to have been at a public school, but the name of it tended to vary and I suspected that it had really been the local comprehensive, just as I suspected that his father, whom he spoke of as a colonel, had at most been a sergeant. The only things about his childhood of which I was sure were that his mother had died young and that he had hated his father with a lasting, unforgiving hatred. What he had to say on that subject never varied and if Felix repeated anything more than two or three times I was generally inclined to believe it. He forgot his own lies so quickly that he was always falling into the trap of contradicting himself and if he did not do this there was a reasonable chance that what he said was true.

"Are all these photographs yours?" I asked, gesturing at the array on the walls.

"Yes, photography's one of my hobbies," Oliver Flint said. "Has it never fascinated you?"

"Oh, I click a camera now and then when I go on holidays, but I just send my films to the chemist to be developed," I answered. "This kind of thing would be quite beyond me. These are very fine."

"I'm delighted you think so," he said. "My wife used to want me to take to it professionally, but I'm afraid that would have spoilt it for me. At present I'm totally free in my choice of subjects and I can work hard at it or drop it for a time, just as I choose, and concentrate on some of my other interests. I paint a little, you know, and write a certain amount."

"Yes, Gavin told me about that," I said.

"I'd have liked to show you some of my paintings, if you

were staying longer. You really have to leave tomorrow, have you?"

"I'm afraid so."

"They're as unlike my photographs as possible. I suppose they reflect the opposite side of my nature. As you like the photographs, I'd be very interested to hear what you'd have to say about the paintings. You might not care for them at all. They're quite abstract. I aim at freedom in them, the greatest freedom of which I'm capable. You see, photography is a very strict discipline. So much of it consists of mastering a purely mechanical technique. It's only when you've done that that the possibility arises of expressing yourself. But it's a great challenge. To be faithful to nature and yet reveal just a little more than the average eye takes in."

If he went on like that, I thought, he would soon bore me, so I was glad when Hannah, who had come to stand at my elbow, said, "Don't you think photography can sometimes be dangerous, Oliver, at least when you move away from safe subjects like flowers? People may not always like what you make of them."

"But I hardly ever photograph anyone but Nora and Rosie," he replied, "and they're both wonderful subjects, totally unself-conscious and cooperative. I'd like to photograph you, Mrs. Freer. I think you'd be pleased with it. You really can't stay on a little longer?"

"Do stay on with us, if you'd like to," Hannah said. "You'd find that being photographed by Oliver is an unforgettable experience."

He gave an oddly uneasy laugh. "You see, Hannah is one of the people whom I failed to please."

"And didn't you admit in the end it wasn't one of your best efforts?" she said.

"Did I? The fact is, Mrs. Freer, I showed Hannah a side of her nature that she prefers to conceal."

"I think it revealed certain things about yourself too,

Oliver. It isn't only beauty that's in the eye of the beholder."

There was no mistaking the gibe in her voice, or the asperity that there had been in his. In fact, I realized a little late, I was being used by the two of them to provide cover for a surprisingly bitter little quarrel. As long as I was there as an audience they could not go too far for the kind of social gathering that we were in, and at the same time I had the feeling that directing their jabs at one another through me gave them both a peculiar kind of pleasure.

Hannah at least, I thought, was enjoying herself, though I was not so sure about Oliver. What had really happened, I wondered, when he had photographed her? Had he made the mistake of trying to make a pass at her and was she reminding him now that she had rejected and successfully humiliated him? It must have been something like that, for at the moment he was certainly the angrier of the two. With another unconvincing laugh he suddenly moved away.

Hannah laughed too.

"Such a phoney, isn't he?" she said. "I can't think how Nora puts up with him, but she seems to be infatuated with him still. It's beyond my understanding."

Nora came to talk to me for a little then, to tell me with pride what a brilliant girl Rosie was. Her plain, innocent face glowed when she spoke of her daughter.

"You'd never guess, from the way she sometimes acts, what a serious person she is," she said. "When she's happy, as she is today, she's like a child, but she got a first in social science and she's been in a very interesting job in Spellbridge in one of the welfare services, working mostly with old people. I'm sure she's wonderful with them. She must be like a breath of fresh air coming into their lives. And she's someone who really cares. There's nothing she won't do for other people. She hasn't given up the job. She's going back to it when they get home from Cornwall."

Hannah had moved away, uninterested.

"Gavin's very lucky," I said.

Nora gave an eager nod. "He is and I'm quite sure he realizes it. I know he worries about the difference in age, but in some ways he's very young, isn't he, and Rosie is more mature than you might think. They're both very much in love, that's the main thing. Tell me, did you know his first wife?"

"Oh yes, quite well," I said.

"She must have hurt him terribly for him to have become so—well, so unsure of himself. He'd known Rosie for two or three years and anyone could see he was in love with her before he could bring himself to ask her to marry him."

"I think he's always been like that," I said. "It's one of the things I like about him."

"Yes, he's so modest, I like that too. But I had to prod him —I wouldn't tell everyone this, but you're such very old friends—I really had to prod him to get on and put the poor girl out of her agony, because Rosie's very innocent, you know, for her generation. She was certain he just thought of her as a nice child and didn't know how to give him the right sort of encouragement. But everything turned out for the best in the end. Oh, please excuse me, there's Paul—Paul Haycock, do you know him?—I must go and say hello to him."

She moved away as a tall man appeared in the doorway.

He was much too tall to come through it without stooping and he did not realize this in time. The crack that he gave his head as he came into the room must have been quite unpleasant. Rubbing his forehead, he swore quietly. Hannah laughed. It occurred to me that she was the kind of person who would laugh if she saw someone slip on a banana skin. It was somehow not out of character that what there was of her almost non-existent sense of humour should be quite crude. But then I remembered, after wondering for a moment why the name seemed familiar, that Paul Haycock was the man who was said to have jilted her. Or whom she had jilted. The true facts of the case were obscure. Also it had been the mention of his name on the telephone that morning that seemed to have upset her father. However, he did not appear discomposed at finding Hannah there, for on hearing her laugh he grinned back at her and after he had apologized to Nora for being late made his way to Hannah's side and gave her a friendly kiss of greeting.

The speeches came soon after that, one by Oliver Flint, which, as Edward Brownlow had predicted, was unnecessarily long and contrived to be mainly about himself, though he mentioned the fact that his daughter was happily not moving far away, as the young Brownlows had taken a flat in Spellbridge. He then proposed their healths, after which Gavin made a brief and stumbling reply, and as soon as it was over Rosie vanished, to reappear after a few minutes with a suitcase.

While she was gone one of the guests said to Oliver, "Why don't the young people put their names down for one of the flats that are going to be built up here? I hear they're going to be quite sumptuous. And Charlwood, even if it isn't what it was, is a good deal more attractive than Spellbridge."

"As a matter of fact, that's our wedding present to them," Oliver replied. "We're buying them one of those flats. But they'll have to wait quite a while for it."

"I've heard work's starting on them in another few weeks," someone said. "Paul, d'you know anything about that?"

Paul Haycock shook his head. He was still standing beside Hannah and after the speeches had been made had been chatting to her in what appeared to be a friendly manner, to which she had responded with as much amiability as was ever to be expected of her.

He was a well-built man, except that he had the beginnings of a paunch, and had the round, florid face of someone who ate and drank well. He had small, bright, dark eyes, set far apart above a short, blunt nose, a wide mouth with fleshy lips, which smiled readily, and thick, sleek brown hair. His age might have been anything between forty and fifty. Gavin, I remembered, had said that he was on the town council, which I thought might explain why he in particular might know something about the building of the flats. Later I heard that he was chairman of the Housing and Development Committee.

However, he said, "It's out of my committee's hands at last, thank God. There's been endless trouble about those flats. I wish we'd never heard of them. The environment crowd have fought them tooth and nail, and I must say I've some sympathy with them. It's sad to see a pretty little place like Charlwood being engulfed by Spellbridge. But you couldn't blame the landowner for wanting to get what he could for that piece of land, which is practically surrounded by building already and no use for anything else, and he's got a lot of local influence and managed to bring some pretty heavy pressure to bear. Anyway, it's going to be a very fine development. We needn't be ashamed of it."

"But it won't improve things here for you, will it, Oliver?" someone else said. "It'll spoil your view and give you rather a feeling of being hemmed in."

"That won't matter much to us," Oliver Flint replied with a laugh. "Nora and I are thinking of selling up and moving to Portugal."

"Selling up—leaving us?" the same person said in a tone of protest. "But that's too bad! I've always thought of you as fixtures. And where will Nora be without her garden?"

"I expect I can have a garden there," she said, "even if we don't sell the things we grow. I'll just have to get used to growing vines instead of cabbages. Perhaps I'll even try my hand at making our own wine."

"This is serious, is it?" Paul Haycock asked. "You're really thinking of moving?"

"Well, thinking about it is really as far as we've got at present," she answered. "I shouldn't have mentioned it if Oliver hadn't. But it would be nice to settle somewhere with a good climate, wouldn't it, and if we don't move soon, I know we never will. I think it's a mistake to leave that sort of thing till you're really old."

"And Oliver will be able to take photographs of all kinds of new things," Hannah said. "He'll enjoy that."

There was mockery in her tone and I saw a flash of the anger that she seemed able to provoke in him cross Oliver's face. But it was just then that Rosie came in with her suitcase and wearing a short fur jacket over her suit. The fur was mink and new, another wedding present, perhaps, as well as the flat that had been promised. It seemed that Nora's inheritance, if it would cover the move to Portugal too, must have been substantial.

Rosie kissed her parents and a number of the guests, Gavin said a general good-bye, picked up her suitcase, then escaped to the car, and Rosie, with her mother's arm round her, followed him.

The crowd of guests flowed out after them. The rain had stopped, but a bitter little wind had risen and dead, sodden leaves fluttered along the ground. There was the first tinge of dusk in the light. As the car started everyone waved and called out good wishes, it disappeared and we all trooped indoors again to have our glasses refilled and to start chatting once more, though with a sense of anticlimax, now that the serious business of the afternoon was over.

But it was some time, as there was still plenty of champagne left, before people started looking at their watches and the first few took their leave. Hannah joined Felix and me, who had drifted together as the numbers thinned in the room.

"We might as well be going," she said. "We'll have to walk home. I didn't bring the car, as it isn't any distance. But it'll be dark soon and I didn't bring a torch."

Paul Haycock overheard her and said, "I'll drive you home."

"Thank you, Paul, but it really isn't necessary," she answered.

"No trouble at all, you know that." He had a deep, self-confident voice. "I'll be driving right past the house in any case, and the road will be disgustingly muddy after all the rain we've had."

"Then come in and have a drink with Father, if you aren't afraid of catching his flu," she suggested. "It'll cheer him up."

"No, I don't think I'll do that, if you don't mind," he said.

"I'm not at all sure the flu is even real," she said. "When we get home I think we may find there's been a miraculous cure. He just didn't want to come here this afternoon. You know how he and Oliver feel about each other."

"I'm not worrying about the flu," Paul Haycock said. "I've got some work waiting for me at home. But let me drive you back."

She accepted the offer this time, to the satisfaction of Felix, who never had much use for exercise even in sunny weather and who would certainly not be at all attracted by the thought of splashing his way through puddles on a cold November afternoon.

The four of us said good-bye to the Flints and went out to Paul Haycock's pale grey Jaguar. Hannah insisted on my taking the front seat, while she and Felix took the seats at the back. The drive to the Brownlows' gateway took about three minutes. The gates were open and Paul Haycock was about to turn the car in at them to drive right up to the house when Hannah stopped him.

"No, just put us down here, Paul," she said, "if you really won't come in. Are you sure you won't?"

He hesitated, then repeated that he had work waiting for him at home.

"But there's something I want to tell you before you go,"

he said. "I'd have told you about it in there if there hadn't been such a confounded lot of noise. It isn't the sort of thing I wanted to shout. And also with Gavin there, I wasn't sure if it was the right time to mention it."

"Why, what's Gavin done now?" she asked.

"Nothing. It isn't that. But the fact is . . . You see, I'm getting married myself." He gave her a swift, anxious look.

"You are?" Strangely enough, in view of the things that Felix and I had been told about her and Paul Haycock, she did not seem at all disturbed. "Is it anyone we know?"

"Well, yes, as it happens, you know her rather well. And that's why I didn't want to talk about it with Gavin there. It's Kay."

"Kay . . . ?" For an instant Hannah sounded bewildered, as if she had no idea who Kay might be. But then she exclaimed, "Kay! I didn't know you even knew her. That's to say, that you knew her well. Of course I knew that you'd met her here when she and Gavin were still together. What a surprise!"

"I thought it might be," he said. He sounded relieved, as if he had been prepared for a different reaction from her. "But we've been seeing a lot of each other during the last year or so and when I was in London last week we decided we'd get married."

"You've been meeting in London, have you?" Hannah said. "But she'll be coming to live here, I suppose."

"Yes, that's the idea."

"I wonder how she'll like it. Won't she think we're all impossibly provincial?"

"She says she thinks it may be a nice change after London," he said. "She says she's tired of London."

Tired too, perhaps, at forty, I thought, of being single and of going on and on working for her living on a glossy women's magazine. She had stuck to her job all the time that she had been married to Gavin and for the last few years since their divorce, but marriage to this apparently prosperous man would at least give her a nice rest.

"I could understand it if you lived somewhere lovely in the country," Hannah said, "but Spellbridge! However, that's her affair. Congratulations, Paul. I hope you'll both be very happy."

Felix and I both added some congratulatory muttering to this and Paul Haycock thanked us.

"But what I really want to know," he said, "is how you think Gavin will take this, Hannah. Will he mind having Kay living so close to him? You know my flat is only just round the corner from the one he and Rosie have taken."

"I don't think he'll care in the least," she answered.

"Are you sure? They're bound to keep running into one another."

"Why should it matter? He's got other interests now." She paused. "Of course, I don't know how Rosie will take it."

"I don't see why she should be jealous, any more than I shall be of Gavin. He's the one I'm not sure about. I've never known what he really felt about that divorce."

"Oh, he wanted it all right. As soon as Kay began to talk of giving up her job and having a baby, as she once told me she did, he started to want a divorce. He wouldn't listen when she said they ought to try to make a new start." The rasp that usually came into Hannah's voice when she spoke of Gavin was audible in it now. "He said for one thing she'd never be faithful—" She stopped abruptly. Never at any time a tactful person, it must have struck even Hannah that to talk of Kay's infidelities to the man she was about to marry was going a little far.

But he laughed. "Oh, I know Kay. But she's done some growing up in recent times. I think there's a good chance we'll make a success of it."

"I hope you do, Paul." She sounded sincere. "Is this news public property, by the way? Can I tell Father about it?"

"If you want to."

"I wonder how he'll take it. She charmed him as well as everyone else. He never believed Gavin's stories about her. When will the wedding be?"

"We haven't decided. Quite soon, I think. Now that we've made up our minds, there's no point in waiting. About Gavin . . ."

"Yes?"

"Oh, nothing. It's just that I've always felt that behind that mild, absent-minded manner of his there are some pretty violent feelings bottled up."

"Then you're one of the few people who's seen through him," Hannah said.

"He doesn't like me, you know."

"That shouldn't matter."

"I hope he's as much in love with Rosie as he seems to be."

Hannah gave a curious chuckle. "I don't think he's in love with her at all. But you needn't be afraid of him." She got out of the car. "Thanks for the lift, Paul. Good-bye."

He said good-bye, added to Felix and me that it had been nice to meet us and we said that it had been nice to meet him, then as soon as we got out of the car he drove off, accelerating swiftly along the country road. The three of us started up the drive. For a moment we walked in silence, then, glancing at Hannah, I saw with a sense of shock that she was convulsed with silent laughter.

That was the first time that I asked myself if she was slightly mad.

"It's all so bloody funny, isn't it?" she said. "You may not see how funny it is, because you aren't an outsider like me. An observer. I see a great deal, you know, of what's going on under the surface. Much more than most people do, because I'm not involved. Paul didn't like my saying that he shouldn't be afraid of Gavin, did you notice that? But he's got every reason to be afraid of him, only he doesn't know I know it. Oh, it's so funny."

I felt a sudden pity for her because of the appalling emptiness of a life such as hers seemed to be, but at the same time I felt angry with her.

"Why did you have to say Gavin doesn't care for Rosie?" I said. "I think he's very much in love with her."

"Don't listen to her, Hannah," Felix said quickly. "When she gets one of her attacks of criticizing people the best thing is not to listen. She was always criticizing me in the old days and I made a point of never listening. What would have been the use? She couldn't have changed me, even if I'd wanted her to, which I didn't, except occasionally. You don't want to change, do you? Why should you?"

He was trying to remove the sting there might have been in what I had said to her, but she exclaimed violently, "You're quite wrong! I'd like to change. I'd like to be a totally different person. But it's too late. They won't let me. I'm too useful to them all as I am. My father and Gavin and everybody . . ." Her voice rose hysterically as she fumbled for her key in her handbag. We had almost reached the house. "Between them they'd destroy me if they weren't afraid of me, but I know so much about them all—" She stopped. She had just noticed the car that was parked in front of the house. "That's Stephen Ledbetter's car," she said in a perfectly calm tone. "I wonder what he's doing here."

As she spoke the door opened. A man stood in the doorway. With the light behind him I could not see much of what he was like, except that he was tall, very thin, narrow-shouldered and gave an impression of age. If he was Stephen Ledbetter, he was the man whose telephone call to Edward Brownlow in the morning had made him change his mind about going to the Flints' reception and that had somehow caused the strange constraint of the lunch in the Golden Fleece.

"Just a minute, Hannah," he said quickly, standing in her way as she was about to go in. "I must warn you, a terrible thing has happened. I won't try to break it gently to you. You're too strong a woman to need it. It's your father. He's— well, he's dead."

A cry broke from Hannah, a single cry. Then she went rigid. I did not think of her myself as a strong woman, but it was an impression that she might make on some people. At that moment it was what she appeared to be.

"Dead?" she said in a harsh voice. "Then he really was ill this morning. And I didn't believe it."

"He may have been ill, I don't know," the old man in the doorway said. "But that isn't what killed him. He was killed by a blow on the head. I've already sent for the police. Now come in, but I warn you, he's just outside your room, in the passage, and it's very horrible."

"Show me," she said.

CHAPTER 4

The room that Stephen Ledbetter had described as Hannah's was next to the kitchen and once, in the days when there had been a staff of servants in the house, might have been the housekeeper's room. I had not been into it, or even seen into it before. A short passage led out of the hall past it to the kitchen, but the evening before, when I had been helping Hannah to clear the table after dinner, the door had been closed.

It was open now and on the floor just outside it lay Edward Brownlow. He was lying on his back with his legs sprawled apart and his arms flung out, as if he had tried to break his fall when he was struck. One eye was staring, the other was hidden by the blood on his face that had gushed from a wound above his forehead. I took it all in in a moment of strange detachment, including the fact that in a desk and a tallboy in the room beyond him drawers had been left open and papers scattered about. Then everything began to waver around me and was almost lost in a grey haze. Stephen Ledbetter caught me by the arm and led me away to the drawing room.

He thrust me into a chair.

"Better now?" he asked.

"Yes," I said. "I'm sorry."

"I imagine you've never seen violent death before. May I ask who you are?"

As it happened, I had seen violent death, but not straight on top of a good deal of champagne, the effects of which had hit me far more strongly than I had expected as soon as I had come out of the Flints' house into the open air.

"I'm Virginia Freer," I said. "My husband and I were witnesses this morning at Gavin's wedding."

"Ah yes, Edward said something about you." He looked about sixty-five and had a stern, worn face with a high, almost pointed forehead from which the grey hair had receded. He had grey eyes behind gold-rimmed spectacles. "My name's Ledbetter—Stephen Ledbetter. I'm the Brownlows' solicitor. I must go to Hannah now. This will be terrible for her. She was exceptionally devoted to her father."

He went out, leaving the door open behind him. I heard him talking in the hall, I supposed to Hannah, then a moment later Felix came in. He was very pale and there were beads of sweat on his forehead.

"Would you believe it, I've just been sick?" he said. "I had to dash out into the garden as fast as I could. God, what a fool it makes me feel!"

I had no difficulty in believing him. Felix had a horror of the sight of blood even more extreme than mine, and I am fairly squeamish.

"It feels cold in here," he went on. "That's nerves, I suppose. I always shiver when I'm upset."

I felt cold myself, no doubt for the same reason, because there were the remains of a good fire in the fireplace. Felix stirred it up with the poker and added a couple of logs from a copper scuttle. They caught quickly and sparks went leaping up the chimney.

"He seems to have been after the silver," I said.

"Who?" Felix asked.

"The murderer, of course. Don't you remember, there was a silver rose bowl on that table there?" I pointed. "And there were two silver vases on the mantelpiece. They're gone too. But I'm sure those two figures—they're Dresden, aren't they? —would be a good deal more valuable than the other things, so he's someone who just has a market for silver. That may help the police narrow the field down a bit. I wonder if he got the forks and spoons. I'd a feeling yesterday evening at dinner that they were Georgian and probably awfully valuable."

But even as I spoke I felt that there was something wrong with what I was saying, though I was still in too much of a state of shock to be able to work out what it was. Just then Hannah and the lawyer came into the room.

Hannah was pale and her eyes looked very big in her stricken face, yet she appeared remarkably calm. She was one of those neurotics, I thought, who can deal with real disaster with far more equanimity than they can with their imaginary fears. The challenge of genuine calamity brings out their strength. People say of them that you can always count on them in a crisis, and so you can for a limited time.

"We must send a message to Gavin," she said. "He and Rosie are breaking their journey at the Great Western Hotel in Exeter. I don't know when they'll get there, but we can leave a message for them. I imagine they'll come straight back."

"I'll see to that now," Ledbetter said. "I suppose I can get the number of the hotel from Enquiries."

"But have a drink first, Stephen," Hannah said. "You look as if you need it. It must have been fearful for you, coming in and finding him like that." She was performing the part of gracious hostess far more effectively than she had the evening before. "By the way, you haven't told me how you managed to get in."

"By the front door," he said. "It wasn't locked."

"Of course," she said. "It's so quiet round here, even with all that building near us, we often don't bother to lock up when there's someone at home."

"I rang," he said, "but there wasn't any answer, so I thought Edward might be asleep, or perhaps in bed. He said something this morning about going down with flu. I was pretty certain he was in, as he was expecting me, so I tried the handle, opened the door and called out to him. Of course there wasn't any answer. So I went looking for him . . . Yes, thank you, Hannah, I'd like a drink."

"Whisky?"

"Please."

She looked at me. "And you?"

Still afloat on a sea of champagne, I almost shuddered. "No, thank you."

Felix said the same.

"But I think I'll deal with that message to Gavin now," Ledbetter said, turning towards the door. "Once the police get here, they'll take charge and it may be some time before we can get it off."

"How soon will they get here?" Hannah asked. "When did you call them?"

"As soon as I found Edward. I suppose that was about a quarter of an hour ago. I should think they'll be here any time now."

He went out and I heard him at the telephone while Hannah poured out his drink.

He had just finished his conversation with someone in the Great Western Hotel in Exeter and had returned and started to drink his whisky when the front doorbell rang and Hannah, dignified and perfectly in command of herself, went to answer it.

It was the police. At first there were only two of them, but soon the house seemed to be full of large men, moving about strangely quietly in obedience to only muttered orders and with such a certainty of what they had to do that it was as if they had been told what it was before they got there.

The man in charge was Detective Superintendent Hoyle, a big, thickset man with a big, square head set on a thick neck, blunt features and smooth, ruddy cheeks. It was easy to imagine him as a younger man in uniform, pounding a beat in one of the less savoury parts of Spellbridge. Although he was in plain clothes, he conferred on them the appearance of uniform. If he had been strolling along the street after he had finished his day's work, or had gone into a pub for a quiet drink, anyone at all knowledgeable would have recognized him at once for what he was.

He asked Hannah, the lawyer, Felix and me to wait in the drawing room while a preliminary examination was made of Edward Brownlow's body and the room in the doorway of which it lay. I gathered that this room was a kind of office from which Hannah managed the affairs of the household. We sat about silently in the drawing room, waiting to be questioned, as we knew that we soon must be, and it was not long before the superintendent came in and asked if he might use the dining room for interviewing us one by one.

As the person who had found the body and reported it to the police, Ledbetter was the first to be asked to go to the drawing room. He and the superintendent seemed to know one another, though their attitude to one another was formal. While the lawyer was gone Hannah sat upright on one of the stiff armchairs with her hands clasped on her knees and a glazed, faraway look in her eyes. She might have been unaware that Felix and I were there in the room with her.

Felix was looking thoughtful in a way that I distrusted. When he looked like that he was often planning something peculiarly imaginative and altogether divorced from the realities of the situation in which he happened to find himself. But he had no need to invent anything to deflect suspicion of the murder, or even of the theft of the silver, from himself, because both he and I had impeccable alibis. From the time that we had left the house in the morning, when Hannah could state that her father had still been alive, we had been in the company of other people until Ledbetter showed us the dead body. But the trouble was that Felix distrusted the truth. He never expected to be believed when he stuck to it. Also he often found it insufficiently colourful to satisfy him and liked to touch it up here and there. I felt inclined to advise him to avoid that on this occasion, but the sight of Hannah rigid, remote and silent, kept me silent too.

It was Hannah who was questioned after Ledbetter. She was out of the room for a far longer time than he. Felix smoked several cigarettes while she was gone and Ledbetter helped himself to another drink. When she returned she dropped into a chair, all the stiffness gone out of her, and said, "I wish someone would make me some strong coffee."

Felix moved quickly to the door. "I'll do it."

"No, no, I didn't mean it," she responded irritably. "I don't want to be any trouble to anyone."

"I think coffee would be good for us all," I said.

"But Felix doesn't know his way around the kitchen," Hannah protested plaintively, as if, when it came to the point, she disliked the thought of anyone else prowling around her domain, handling her possessions. She began to get to her feet. "I'll do it, if you'd all like it." She managed to sound aggrieved, as if an unreasonable demand had been made upon her. "But they won't let us go down the passage to the kitchen."

"It's all right, Felix can go round outside the house to the back door," I said. "He's very good at finding his way about. And he makes very good coffee. You stay where you are."

She sat down again with an air of unwillingness and Felix went out.

A moment later a constable appeared in the doorway and said that Superintendent Hoyle would like to see me.

As I went towards the dining room I found a number of men, some in uniform, some in plain clothes, standing about in the hall. A man with a camera had just arrived. In the dining room I found the superintendent sitting at one end of the long table, with a younger man sitting on his left with an open notebook before him. Mr. Hoyle indicated a chair on his right.

"Come and sit down, Mrs.—" He consulted some notes on the table. "Mrs. Freer, isn't it? I believe you're a guest here, staying in the house."

"Yes," I replied, sitting down. "I arrived yesterday and I'm going home tomorrow—that is, if I'm not needed here."

"Just so." He had a hoarse yet not unpleasant voice with the flatness of the local accent in it. "Now I'd like you to give Sergeant Gresham your full name, age, home address and occupation."

I did this and saw the sergeant write down what I told him.

"Have you known the Brownlow family long?" Mr. Hoyle asked next.

"I've known Gavin Brownlow for a number of years," I answered. "I've met Miss Brownlow a few times and I met Mr. Brownlow for the first time yesterday."

"This Gavin Brownlow to whom you refer got married today, I believe," he said.

I nodded. "Yes, my husband and I came here to be witnesses at his wedding."

"Not a very happy wedding day for him," he said. "I believe you and your husband are separated."

So Hannah had told him that. I again said, "Yes."

"But do I understand that you both knew Gavin Brownlow when he was married to his first wife?"

"Yes. As a matter of fact, we were witnesses at their wedding too. We weren't separated then."

"That was in London?"

"Yes." I was puzzled by this line of questioning. The questions seemed unimportant. But perhaps they would lead up to something more significant presently. "Gavin hadn't gone into his father's firm yet. He was trying to get started on his own, but he wasn't very successful."

"What did he and his wife live on, then?"

"I think he had some money of his own which he'd inherited from his mother. I don't think it was much, but when you're young you don't much mind that."

"And when it ran out, he came back home?"

"Perhaps. I don't know what his reasons were."

"How much of today were you with him?"

So that was what he had been aiming at. Gavin's alibi, and even a possible motive for murdering his father. I gave him an incredulous stare. Did he think it was possible that Gavin and Rosie should have left the reception, returned to this house, murdered his father, stolen some silver and departed on their honeymoon? Yet this was the point to which his earlier questions had been leading.

"We were together nearly all day," I said. "He and my husband and I set off by car from this house at around half past eleven, went and picked up Miss Flint, drove to the register office in Spellbridge, where they got married, went to the Golden Fleece for lunch, then drove on to the Flints' house for the reception. Now he and his wife are on the way to Cornwall, breaking the journey, I believe, in Exeter. Mr. Ledbetter's sent a message to their hotel there to tell them what's happened."

"So I understand. But can you tell me at what time the two young Brownlows left the reception?" Seeing my expression, he went on with a bland smile, "We like to get things tidied up, Mrs. Freer. It helps in the end, however improbable it may sound. Do you know what time they left the Flints' house?"

"I wasn't watching the clock," I answered. "My guess is it was about four o'clock or soon after."

"That's only a guess?"

"Oh yes."

As he was pondering this, apparently considering his next question, I put one to him. "Do you know when Mr. Brownlow was killed?"

"We can only make a guess at that ourselves," he said. "Perhaps we'll be able to be a little more definite after the post-mortem. At present all we're prepared to say is that it was probably between half past two and half past three. According to Miss Brownlow, she and her father had lunch together at one o'clock, so we may be able to tell a certain amount by the contents of his stomach, and we think he had been dead for well over an hour at the time Mr. Ledbetter says he found him, which was at five o'clock."

"Of course you know some silver's disappeared," I said.

He gave me the bland smile again. "Oh yes, we know that."

"I assume it's been stolen," I said. "All the same . . ." I had just realized why I had felt that there was something wrong with what I had said to Felix about the murderer having been after the silver. "All the same, someone was searching for something else, weren't they? I had a glimpse into Miss Brownlow's room and I saw that the drawers of the desk and the tallboy were open and that papers were scattered around. It isn't likely that a thief would expect to find silver in those drawers, is it? So doesn't it look as if the silver was taken as a blind after the murder, to make it look as if the murderer was an ordinary thief who was caught by Mr. Brownlow, when whoever it was was really hunting for something else?"

"You're reading my mind, Mrs. Freer." It was ironic, but he went on seriously, "Naturally that's something we've got to consider, but it would be a mistake to be too positive about it at this stage. There are other possibilities. One is that two people came into the house this afternoon, one who stole the silver and one who searched Miss Brownlow's room. And if that happened, either of them might have been the murderer."

"Wouldn't that be rather too much of a coincidence?"

"Coincidences happen. Utterly unbelievable coincidences.

And in this case it might not be as much of a coincidence as you think. A good many people must have supposed that this house was going to be empty this afternoon. I understand from Miss Brownlow that Mr. Brownlow only changed his mind about going to the reception during the morning. So anyone who knew about the wedding and the reception would have expected the place to be empty. And I imagine the whole village knew about it and perhaps the word got to certain people in Spellbridge. We've got our villains there, like everyone else. And they'd know that this house would be worth burgling. So it really isn't impossible that two people came into the house for two quite different reasons."

"And that's what you really think?"

He shrugged his heavy shoulders. "I haven't got to the stage of thinking anything yet. There's just one rather definite thing in your theory that taking the silver was a blind. There's a fair sum of money, about two hundred pounds, in the wallet in Mr. Brownlow's pocket. A thief who specializes in silver might not take other valuables, but he wouldn't be likely to leave ready cash behind. But even that's not impossible. He might be a man who isn't normally violent and if he did the murder in a fit of panic might have been too frightened to stay and search the body. And the same thing might hold even if he wasn't the murderer, but came into the house and stumbled over a dead man."

"What weapon did he use?" I asked.

"The good old common or garden poker," he answered. "The blunt instrument most of us have lying to hand in half the rooms in our houses. Unfortunately there aren't any fingerprints on it. He was collected enough to wipe it clean."

"So he didn't bring a weapon with him," I said. "He wasn't expecting to do a murder."

"That's how it looks. As I said, the chances are he was sure the house would be empty. Now there's just one more thing I want to ask you." He put his elbows on the table and leant forward on them, bringing his big face close to mine. "Since you've been here, have you seen anything—anything at all—in the relationships of the people you've met which you've felt was—well, not wholly normal? Anything, in fact, which could throw any light on the motive for this murder?"

Because I did not answer at once, he added, "Anything you say will be treated as confidential, unless it becomes necessary to repeat it."

I was in a quandary, for Hannah, it seemed to me, was far from normal. As we had walked up the drive together after Paul Haycock had driven off and she had had her fit of silent laughter, I had even wondered about her sanity. But in her general dislike of the human race, her father had seemed to be the one exception, and if, in her exclusive love for him, there was something unnatural, was it of the kind which, if it was hurt by jealousy or some slight from him, could all of a sudden turn murderous? I did not know and it would have been very complicated to try to explain. I shook my head.

"I can't think of anything," I said.

"You're sure?"

"I told you," I said, "I've only been here since yesterday and I'd never met Mr. Brownlow before. I don't know anything about his relationships with anyone else."

"Just so. Well, if you should think of anything later, even if it doesn't seem particularly important, will you please tell me about it? Something may occur to you that you hardly noticed at the time. Don't be afraid to speak about it. You never know what may be useful."

It was dismissal. There remained only Felix to be questioned.

I was afraid that he would not enjoy it. Although he had never been in actual trouble with the police, he had been on the edge of it more than once and his attitude to them was wary in the extreme. He could not understand my feeling that on the whole they were on my side and that it was only when

I had committed, say, some minor parking offence or forgotten to renew the registration of my car that I preferred not to see them around. To Felix they were always the enemy, representatives of authority which, beginning with his father, he had fought against all his life.

I was glad that he had made the coffee before he was called in for his questioning. Hannah poured out a cup for me. Taking it, I sat down near the fire, gradually relaxing after the tension of the interview. The hot coffee was consoling. Hannah gazed sightlessly into the fire. Her face was very pale and her eyes looked sunken, but there was no sign in them that she had wept. So far as I knew, she had not yet shed a single tear for her father.

Stephen Ledbetter, a cup of coffee in his hand, was standing with his back to one of the windows. His image was reflected in it, tall, angular and narrow, but beyond it there was only darkness. I thought that he would have looked well in a monk's habit. There was an air of deep austerity about his stern, tired face.

Hannah stirred suddenly, looking towards him.

"I wish you'd draw the curtains, Stephen," she said. "I feel as if there are monsters in the garden, looking in at us."

I had rather the same feeling. There was something eerie about the shiny blackness of the windows. Anything might be lurking out there.

Ledbetter went from window to window, drawing the curtains.

"The monsters have gone," he said. "You aren't afraid of them, are you, Hannah?"

There was more kindliness in his voice than showed in his face.

"Why should I be afraid?" she asked.

"Someone came searching for something in that room of

yours," he said. "I'm wondering if he found it, or if he might
come back. Also I'm wondering what it was."

"So am I," she said.

"You can't think what it could have been?"

"Money, I suppose. I can't think of anything else."

I drank some of my coffee. "That detective told me the
money in your father's wallet wasn't taken."

"I know," she said. "He told me that too."

"Did you keep money in your room, Hannah?" Ledbetter
asked.

"Sometimes, not often. There wasn't any there today. But
he may have thought there might be." Her gaze had gone
back to the fire. "Stephen . . ."

"Yes, my dear?"

"You haven't told us why you came here today. Why did
you?"

He gave a sigh. "I've told the police."

"Do you mind telling me?"

"It was simply because Edward asked me to come."

"Do you know why?"

"Only roughly. Edward said something about wanting to
change his will."

"When was that?"

"A few days ago."

"Why should he want to change it?" Hannah asked. "His
old will, which he told Gavin and me about years ago, left everything he had equally divided between us. I can't think why
he should want to alter that. He'd no one else to leave anything to."

"Perhaps he wanted to make some provision for Kay. He
was very fond of her, you know, and with Gavin getting married again and taking on other obligations, Edward may have
thought he ought to put something aside for her."

Hannah gave her abrupt laugh. "Kay's taken care of that

by herself. Paul told us only this evening that he and Kay are getting married."

I thought that Ledbetter gave a start. Coming forward, he sat down in a chair facing the fire. The reflections in his gold-rimmed glasses of the leaping flames concealed his eyes, but his mouth had grown tight.

"That's an extraordinary thing," he said. He held out his cup. "May I have some more coffee, please?"

It was the action of someone who wanted a moment to think.

Hannah reached out for the coffeepot and refilled his cup.

He went on, "Of course, I may have been wrong about what Edward wanted to do. That was only a guess."

"Is it what you told the police?"

"No, I only told them that Edward mentioned changing his will. They wouldn't find a mere guess particularly helpful."

"I wonder why he didn't go to your office, instead of asking you to come here," she said.

Felix, returning to the drawing room then, heard the question but, before the lawyer could answer it, said, "I think I ought to warn you, Hannah, they've come for your father. I don't suppose you want to see him again before they take him away."

She shut her eyes for a moment, then said in a low voice, "Why should I?"

"Why indeed." Felix said. "I thought that's how you'd feel, but that policeman seemed to think someone ought to ask you."

"It isn't my father out there anymore," she said. "He's gone already. When are all those men going to go?"

"Some of them left a little while ago," Felix answered, "but the boss man isn't showing any signs of moving. A couple of men are searching your room. I wonder if that's legal, if they haven't a search warrant."

"It's all right, I told them they could do what they liked,"

Hannah said indifferently. She turned back to Ledbetter. "Why didn't Father go to your office, Stephen? That's what he usually did if he'd business with you, isn't it?"

"Yes, and I was expecting him this morning," he replied. "But he didn't come, so I rang up his office first and was told he hadn't arrived there, so then I rang up here, as you know, and he told me about having flu and asked me to come here. I asked him if it was really urgent and he insisted it was, so I came. I only wish I'd come sooner. It might have saved him."

"Or you might both be dead," Felix suggested.

The lawyer gave him a startled look.

Felix went on, "On the other hand, I gather the police think the murderer didn't come here to kill, as he didn't seem to have brought a weapon, but just grabbed the poker when he was caught doing whatever it was he was doing, so you may be right. If there'd been two of you, perhaps you could have overcome him, even if he was young and active."

"What I don't understand," I said, "is why there should be anything urgent about changing a will. So urgent that Mr. Brownlow cancelled going to the reception this afternoon and stayed at home to do it. He wasn't expecting to die this afternoon."

"Is that why he stayed at home?" Felix asked. "To change his will?"

"So he said," Ledbetter answered. "I've just been explaining to Hannah that that's why I came. But like you, Mrs. Freer, I find it difficult to understand why the matter should be so urgent."

Hannah gave a shrug of her shoulders. "It's what he was like, you know. If he thought of something he wanted to do, he always had to do it immediately. If he'd decided to change his will, he'd want to do it on the spot. You didn't know him as well as I did, Stephen. You may not have seen that side of him."

"You don't suppose . . ." Felix began and stopped.

I would have liked to silence him because I knew the look on his face. He had just had some wild idea which fascinated and convinced him, at least temporarily, but which would only bring confusion into a rational discussion. But both Hannah and Stephen Ledbetter had turned their heads towards him and were waiting for him to go on. Neither of them had discovered yet that he was a dangerous person to take seriously.

"I was just wondering," he said thoughtfully, "if it was possible that Mr. Brownlow knew he might die at any time."

"You mean that he'd just found out he'd some serious illness?" Hannah said. "No, that isn't likely. He always told me if he was going to see his doctor. In fact, I usually had to make the appointment for him. And he hasn't been near him recently. His health was excellent for his age."

"It's a thought, all the same," Ledbetter said. "You know, Hannah, if Edward had got scared about himself, if he'd had pains in his chest, for instance, which he was afraid might mean heart trouble, or those sort of internal pains which people of his age are liable to feel sure are cancer, then he might have kept it from you and gone to see his doctor quietly on his own. And if the verdict was bad, he might have thought he ought to make this change he wanted in his will immediately. You say yourself that anything he wanted done had to be done at once. If that's how it was, it explains a good deal. I think you may have got to the truth of the matter, Mr. Freer."

"As a matter of fact, that isn't what I meant, though I see it's possible," Felix said. "What I was actually wondering about was whether Mr. Brownlow had a quite different sort of reason for fearing for his life. In other words, had he been threatened? Had he some enemy who he knew was dangerous? Someone who thought he'd been injured by Mr. Brownlow and wanted revenge, or someone who'd some reason to be afraid of him. It might be someone who's not quite sane."

"My father never injured anybody," Hannah said sharply.

"Which of us hasn't, even if we never meant to?" the lawyer said. "But I think my explanation's more likely than yours, Mr. Freer."

"Of course, we could both be wrong," Felix said. "There are still all kinds of possibilities—"

He broke off as the sound of the front doorbell pealed through the house.

None of us moved to answer it. We all assumed that whoever had come to the house was someone connected with the police and that it was for them to answer the door. One of them must have gone to it, for we heard voices in the hall, but one of the voices was a woman's, so unless for some reason a woman policeman had been brought on the scene, which seemed unlikely, the visitors might have nothing to do with the police after all.

But they were kept talking in the hall for some minutes before the drawing-room door was opened by a young constable, who looked in and said, "Miss Brownlow, there's a Mr. and Mrs. Flint here who've come to see you, but they aren't sure if you'll want to see them at the moment."

However, almost before he had finished, Nora Flint came rapidly into the room with both hands outstretched. Her husband lingered in the doorway.

"Hannah dear, what a terrible, terrible thing!" Nora Flint cried. "We saw all those police cars and we couldn't think what had happened, or what we ought to do—should we keep out of your way and not be a nuisance, or should we come and see if we could help? And in the end we decided to come, because you can always send us away if you'd sooner we didn't stay, but at least it shows that we care. Oh, my dear, I can't tell you how distressed we are!"

Hannah had stood up the moment the Flints came into the room. She did not even look at Nora and, ignoring her outstretched hands, went to the door, brushed past Oliver as if he were not there and disappeared from the room. I heard her suddenly break into a run as she went rushing up the stairs.

CHAPTER 5

Still in the doorway, Oliver Flint said, "I told you we shouldn't have come."

Nora Flint was looking after Hannah in dismay. "Yes, it was a mistake, wasn't it?" She turned to me. "Is there anything we can do to help? You're staying here, aren't you? If you aren't, Hannah could come over to spend the night with us. I can't bear the thought that she might be left alone in this great house after what's happened."

"Hannah likes to be alone," Oliver said. "Let's go."

I said, "Felix and I are staying here, at least for tonight."

"We'll go, then," Nora said. "But you'll get in touch with us, won't you, if you think of anything we can do for the poor girl? It's so awful, she was so completely devoted to her father. I don't suppose she's taken things in yet properly. She looked to me in a state of shock. It'll be worse for her when she comes out of it."

"Are you coming?" Oliver asked impatiently. "There's nothing you can do for her."

"No, I know," Nora answered. "I wish there were. It feels so callous, just leaving her."

"She hardly welcomed us."

Nora went towards the door. But it was just then that one of the policemen came in and said that, since they were here, Superintendent Hoyle would like a few words with Mr. and Mrs. Flint.

Oliver said, "Of course," and they were moving together towards the dining room when the constable said that the su-

perintendent would prefer to see them one at a time. Oliver
went first and Nora returned to the drawing room.

Sitting down to wait, her plain, ruddy face creased with
concern, she said, "I'm so glad you're here, Mr. Ledbetter.
Hannah's always had such a regard for you. She sent for you
at once, I suppose, when she found her father. That was sensible of her. You can cope with the police and make sure they
don't overdo the questioning when she isn't fit for it. Have
you thought of calling in Dr. Black? He might give her a sed-
ative and make sure they leave her alone."

"I think they've been quite gentle with her," Stephen Ledbetter answered. "But she didn't send for me. I had an appointment here with Edward this afternoon and arrived a little while before she returned from the reception. So actually
it was I who found him and I was able to break the news of
his death to her. She didn't stumble over his body herself. She
was spared that."

"It must have been a dreadful experience for you, finding
him," she said. "I can't imagine what it felt like. Nothing like
it has ever happened to me. I've never had to have anything
to do with violence. I'm desperately sorry for Hannah, and of
course for Gavin too. And for Rosie. Oh, my poor darling,
what a wedding day! Do she and Gavin know about it yet?
Have they got to know? Couldn't they have just a little time
to themselves before they have to be told?"

"I've already telephoned their hotel in Exeter," Ledbetter
said. "I don't know if they've got the message yet, but I don't
think it would have been possible to delay it."

"Of course not, I'm being stupid," Nora said. "I didn't really mean it. It's just that when I think of Rosie, how happy
she was, how much she's in love with Gavin—well, it takes me
back to when I married Oliver. It was a lovely wedding and
we went to Venice for our honeymoon and everything was absolutely perfect. And now my poor girl isn't going to have a
honeymoon at all and she's going to have to face up to a

murder and try to comfort Gavin. And she's so young to be faced by anything so dreadful."

Felix lit another cigarette. "In my opinion the young can cope with this kind of thing ever so much better than us elderly folk. I remember the blitz on London when I was still a child. My mother used to play cards with me to keep my mind off what was happening. My father was away in the army, of course, so there were just the two of us and I imagine she was pretty frightened, though she put a brave face on things for my sake. But really I found it wonderfully exciting. I loved the loud bangs and the pitch-darkness with just the searchlights in the sky. Even when our windows were blown in and our ceilings came down, I felt it was all part of a tremendous adventure. So I really shouldn't worry too much about your daughter. She won't be nearly as upset as you think."

There were several things the matter with this story. At the time of the blitz on London Felix had been about one year old and certainly had no memories of it at all. He had often told me too that he had no memories of his mother. However, the intention of what he had said, which was to reassure Nora Flint about the probable toughness of her daughter, was a kindly one, so it seemed unnecessary to cast doubts upon it. But I saw Ledbetter give Felix a thoughtful look, as if he were assessing his age and had just begun to wonder what kind of person he was.

"And you really weren't too terribly upset by the raids?" Nora Flint said.

"Not as I should be now," Felix answered, and I wondered if he would go on and add the truth that today's murder had made him vomit, but he did not. "My impression of Rosie is that she's a healthy, intelligent, warmhearted girl who'll be far too concerned about Gavin's feelings to worry about a spoilt honeymoon. After all, that can always come later."

Nora drew a long breath and let it out slowly. "Yes, I'm

sure you're right. It's Gavin she'll think about, not herself. That's what she's like."

"What were her feelings about Edward?" Ledbetter asked. "Will his death mean much to her?"

Edward Brownlow had said that Rosie disliked him. But it is possible to grieve after a fashion over the death of someone one does not like, or even has never met, even if this is only a form of grieving over the inevitability of one's own death. In some people it can be a quite potent emotion.

Nora looked uncertain. "He wasn't really very nice to her, you know. If you want the truth, he was never very nice to any of us. If it hadn't been for Gavin and Rosie I don't suppose we'd ever have seen much of him, even though we were such close neighbours. He and Oliver disagreed about everything. And it's difficult to like a person who doesn't like you. But Rosie always said it would be all right once he got used to her. Well, anyway, she and Gavin were safely away when the poor man was killed, so the police won't trouble them with too many questions. I'm so glad of that. Do you know if they can tell yet when the murder happened?"

"They seem to think it was between half past two and half past three," I said, "though naturally that's only approximate."

I did not tell her that the police had been disturbingly curious about the time when Rosie and Gavin had left the reception.

"They'll ask us for our alibis, I suppose," she said. "They'll be asking everyone, won't they? I'm afraid Oliver hasn't got one. He went out to his darkroom after lunch and stayed there till our first guests arrived. The darkroom's in a sort of barn behind the house, next to where we keep the cultivator and the tools and all, so he could have slipped out without anyone seeing. I was with Hannah, who came to help me, and . . . Oh no!" Her hand went to her mouth. "I was with her for a little while, but then there was the time when I went upstairs to change. Usually, when I change, it only takes me a few minutes, but today I felt I ought to make a special effort and I put on a dress I bought only last week, a thing with a rather bright red and green pattern, and some high-heeled shoes that I hardly ever wear, and a bit of make-up. And when I'd finished I simply hated the sight of myself—I didn't feel it was me, you know—and I took it all off and put on this dress that I've had for years and my usual shoes and felt much better like that. So I suppose I may have been upstairs for almost half an hour and Hannah won't really be able to say where I was or what I was doing."

"Are you sure where she was during that time?" I asked. "If she couldn't see you, I imagine you couldn't see her."

"No, but when I came down I found she'd arranged the glasses and everything for me in the sitting room. She'd been quite busy, so she must have been there."

"What time did she arrive at your house?" I went on.

"I'm not sure. About half past two, I think. So if the murder didn't happen till half past two, she's got an alibi, hasn't she?"

"Not really, because, as I said, that time is only approximate. When did the first guests arrive?"

"About three. I do see that theoretically Oliver or I had time to slip over here after Hannah arrived and before the first of them got there. But of course that's nonsense. All the same, I see I'll have to tell the police about it. It's always best to tell them everything, isn't it?"

"Always," Felix assured her earnestly.

Stephen Ledbetter joined in the questioning of Nora. "I suppose you knew Mr. Brownlow was at home, that he wasn't coming to the reception, Mrs. Flint?"

"Oh yes, Hannah told me," Nora answered. "She said he was unwell."

"But your husband didn't know that," he said, "if he was in his darkroom when Hannah arrived."

She looked thoughtful. "Yes, that's quite right. Until Hannah told me about his flu we both took for granted he'd gone to the office as usual and would be coming straight here from Spellbridge. I know he didn't usually come home for lunch."

"And a lot of other people will have thought that too, I expect. They'll have taken for granted the house would be empty." He gave a grim smile. "I haven't a trace of an alibi myself. I had lunch in my club, then took some work home and stayed there till I drove out here for my appointment with Edward. So unless someone noticed my car when I was on my way here, I've no means of proving that I didn't arrive at the house much earlier than I told the police."

"Do you live alone then?" I asked. It had not occurred to me to wonder whether or not he was married.

"Yes," he answered. "My wife died ten years ago and my son has a job in Toronto and my daughter's married and lives in Glasgow. A woman comes in every morning to clean my flat and she leaves something prepared for my evening meal, but she's always gone by twelve o'clock, so there's no one to corroborate that I was really in the flat. I've admitted as much to the police. But Hoyle and I have known each other for years. I think the chances are that he believes me. But he's a cunning man behind that bluff exterior. It's difficult to be sure what he's thinking. And I've always heard that the first person to be suspected, after the immediate family, is the person who reports the discovery of the body."

Nora looked interested. "Is that really so? How very strange. But they couldn't suspect you, Mr. Ledbetter, I'm sure they couldn't. You're so well known in Spellbridge. But they can't suspect the immediate family either. Gavin was with Rosie, so it couldn't possibly have been him, and Hannah, as we all know, adored her father."

"And how could she have got rid of the silver?" I said. "I don't think she'd have had the time to dump it, and anyway, she wouldn't have risked hiding it near the house."

"Silver?" Nora said. "Has some silver been stolen?"

I told her about it briefly. As I did so I noticed a curious look appear on Felix's face. It was the one that I thought of as his guilty look. Unfortunately for him, his face betrayed his feelings very easily, at least to someone who knew him as well as I did. Perhaps to someone who did not his present expression might simply have signified a loss of interest in what we were talking about, a desire to change the subject, but to me it meant an attempt at concealment of some sudden, acute uneasiness. It was something to do with the silver, I thought, something that had just occurred to him about its disappearance, and I made up my mind to question him about it as soon as we found ourselves alone together.

But that was not to be yet, though Stephen Ledbetter soon afterwards obtained permission from Superintendent Hoyle to go home. Leaving, he said that if Hannah should want him he would of course return, but that he thought that I could probably do more for her at present than he could. Then, when the superintendent had finished with Oliver Flint, Nora was asked to go into the dining room and Oliver joined Felix and me in the drawing room.

Asking Felix for a cigarette, he started looking here and there about the room, as if he were searching for something, and Felix, divining without difficulty what it was, poured him out a drink.

"Thanks," Oliver said, taking it and sitting down, stretching his long legs out before him and crossing his ankles. "All the emotion in the atmosphere takes it out of one."

"Don't tell us you found Superintendent Hoyle emotional," Felix said. "A very stolid character, I thought."

"I'm thinking of myself," Oliver replied. I ought to have guessed, from the little that I knew of him, that that was what he would be doing. "I find I can't take murder in my stride, even when the victim's a man I'd no use for at all. It scares me. Irrational, isn't it? But I really got frightened, talking to Hoyle, because I haven't any kind of alibi. Then there's the way Hannah acted when Nora and I came in. Why did she do that? Does she think one of us could have had anything to do with it? Is she going to try to drag us into it, simply because her father didn't like us? And d'you know why he didn't? Has she told you that?"

The lines of tension on his face were deeper than when I had seen him last. He was genuinely upset on his own account, if not on that of anyone else.

"No," I said.

"He was a snob. A success and money snob. He despised us because we chose to live in a way that gave both of us real satisfaction and didn't spend our energies on a lot of the cheap sort of ambitions he understood. It upset him, as if it was a criticism of him, that we didn't care about money. But why should we? We'd the market garden—that's Nora's passion in life—and I'd my other interests too. We're two very contented people, and he couldn't stand that. When we first came to live here he tried to patronize us, but when we showed that didn't go down with us he became so offensive that we did our best to have nothing to do with him. Then the joke of it was that Nora inherited quite a lot of money, so it was our turn to be offensive. Well, not offensive, because we didn't want to spoil things for Gavin and Rosie, but I've never been good at hiding my feelings and I made it plain to Brownlow what I thought of his shoddy values. He never forgave me and unluckily Hannah never did either. She's fairly good friends with Nora, but she can't stand the sight of me. That's why I didn't want to come here this evening. . . ." He swallowed most of his whisky. "Ah well, I oughtn't to be talking about the poor devil like this. Let's talk about something else. I imagine you won't be going home tomorrow after all, Virginia."

"If the police want me to stay, I suppose I shall have to," I said.

"Then why not come down to my studio sometime and let me photograph you, as I suggested? I think I could make something of it."

Being photographed is one of the easiest ways of which I know of being reduced to total misery. I shook my head.

"But why not try Felix?" I said. "He'd be a far more interesting subject."

This was mean of me, because Felix has an even worse phobia than I have about being photographed, though it is for a different reason. Mine is simply vanity. Someone has only to point a camera at me to start me looking my worst. The results invariably horrify me. Felix, on the other hand, is extremely photogenic. He faces the camera with a delightful smile and an appearance of immensely enjoying himself. All the same, he has a curious fear of it. Sooner or later, he seems to feel, the photograph will get into the hands of people, the police, for instance, who will be able to use it against him. Someday, he may think, he will go that little bit too far along the road of minor crime and find them after him, and then, if they can find a good photograph of him, it could be dangerous.

Oliver turned to Felix and looked him up and down with a thoughtful stare in which I saw in him for the first time the gaze of the pure professional. It gave character to his handsome but not very expressive face. I thought that this might be the first time that I was seeing the real Oliver. Then he nodded.

"What about it?" he said. "I'll be doing it for my own pleasure. It won't cost you anything."

To my surprise, Felix said, "If you like, if I'm still here tomorrow."

"Your wife's right, I think it would be interesting," Oliver said. "Say about eleven o'clock, then."

"I'd better telephone," Felix replied. "After all, I may be leaving, and even if I'm not, I don't know when I'll be free."

"Right, telephone. I'll be at home all day." Oliver got to his feet as Nora came into the room. "Are they finished with us?" he asked.

"Yes, we can go." She turned to me. "When Rosie and Gavin get back, you'll tell them they can stay with us, won't you? I don't like the thought of Rosie having to stay in this house after what's happened here. And it won't help Hannah, having them here. She doesn't like either of them. Good night."

"Good night," I answered.

She and Oliver left.

As the door closed behind them, Felix stooped and put another log on the fire.

I asked, "Are you really going to telephone Oliver tomorrow and let him photograph you?"

"Why not?" he said.

"Because you're usually so neurotic about being photographed."

"And you never thought I'd agree, that's why you suggested it." He grinned. "Well, you're often wrong about me."

"But just why did you agree?" I asked.

"I thought I'd like to investigate his studio. Photographers are often rather sinister people, anyway in books. They keep all sorts of poisons lying around."

"But this isn't a case of poisoning. There's no question of that. Why did you really agree?"

"I thought I'd like to see a little more of the man. He's scared, you know."

"Yes, I rather had that feeling myself," I said, "though I don't see why he should be. There are several people besides him who haven't got alibis. They can't all be involved in the murder."

"What did you think about that man, Haycock, who drove

us home? He came late to the party. He might have come to this house first."

"I don't know anything about him. All I know is, you and I are absolutely above suspicion. We've been under observation all day. You know, that gives me a queer feeling of being outside the whole thing, just looking in at it."

"What it makes me feel is rather smug," Felix said. "Even you can't have any doubts about me. That's a nice change."

"I've never suspected you of violence," I said. "In some ways I think you'd be more normal if you were more aggressive. It's when things mysteriously disappear when you're in the neighbourhood that I start to worry. That silver, now."

He started. His gaze had been on a charming little Steuben owl on the mantelpiece, just the right size to slip easily into one of his pockets. He looked puzzled.

"The silver? What on earth could I have done with that?"

"That's what I'd like to know."

"Now look here," he protested, "whatever else I may be, and you always tend to exaggerate my failings, I'm not a magician. You've been with me yourself all day. How could I possibly have nicked a rose bowl, some vases and a great case of Georgian silver? When could I have helped myself to them and where could I have hidden them?"

"So he did get the forks and spoons," I said.

"So Hoyle told me."

"Well, I don't admit that I exaggerate what you're capable of, in fact, I think I often play it down out of a sort of habit of trying to save you from yourself, but I haven't suggested you took the silver. I know you aren't a magician, and so far as I know, you've never stolen from your friends. It's in shops that you can't control yourself when something takes your fancy, and that's so impersonal, I don't believe you think of it as stealing."

"What are you suggesting, then?"

He ought to have been looking offended. It would have

been only natural if he had been innocent. But he was looking merely indifferent and aloof. It was almost the same look as I had seen on his face a little earlier, the one that I thought of as his guilty look, which had made me think that he knew something about the silver.

"Just that when we were talking about it a little while ago," I said, "I thought some idea came suddenly into your head about what might have happened to the stuff."

He shook his head. "You've always had this notion that you know more about me than I do myself. How could I know anything about what happened?"

"Well, suppose you'd remembered having talked to one of your less savoury friends who happened to come from Spellbridge, or anyway who knew a good deal about the place, about how you were coming here to this wedding and about the reception we were all going to and so on. Someone who took a surprising amount of interest in what you were saying and asked you a lot of questions about it. Someone who gathered from you that the house would be empty for the afternoon and who also happened to specialize in silver. If he knew this neighbourhood well, he might have known there was some valuable stuff to be picked up here. Was there anyone like that?"

"And you always complain that I've too much imagination for my own good!" he exclaimed.

"Am I right, though? Was there anyone like that?"

He fidgeted. "Suppose there was."

"Who was it?"

"No one you know."

"I don't imagine it was. One of the advantages of our separation has been that I don't have to try to put up with some of the odd characters you seem to like. I never much enjoyed the feeling of not being sure whether the person you were introducing me to was an eminent fellow of the Royal Society or a pickpocket."

"I could name one who was both," he said. "A remarkable man. But you'd have been too narrow-minded to appreciate him. He was a brilliant physicist and at the same time he'd the neatest set of fingers of anyone I've ever known. Going out with him for an evening was an education in itself. I remember—"

I interrupted. "You're trying to change the subject, and anyway, I'm sure he never existed. About this friend of yours who questioned you about the silver—"

"He never said a word about silver."

"No, I suppose he wouldn't. But this man, whoever he was, who wanted to know a lot about the wedding and about what the family were going to be doing—oughtn't you to tell the police about him?"

"Why?"

"Why? Oh, my God, Felix, don't you realize he's probably the murderer?"

"Most unlikely," he said. "If the man I'm thinking of did come here and take the silver, and mind you, it's only a guess that that's who it was, and I don't want to get someone into trouble simply because he was taking a friendly interest in why I was coming to a place like Spellbridge, then I'm quite sure he wasn't the murderer. Murder isn't his line. People like him, real professionals, don't suddenly take to violence if they don't normally go in for it. If he'd wanted to knock Brownlow out so that he could get away, he'd have known how to hit him without doing any real damage."

"He could have made a mistake just for once. Suppose Brownlow's skull is abnormally thin, or something like that. And even if this man isn't the murderer, I still think you ought to tell the police about him. Apart from the fact that they sometimes like to catch burglars, he may even have seen something. He may be able to tell them something important."

Felix again stubbornly shook his head. "No, I don't really know anything."

"Well, if you won't tell them about him, I shall."

He gave me a sly smile. "But what have you got to tell them, my love? That you noticed a peculiar expression on my face? They probably think my face is peculiar anyway. I often think so myself when I look at myself in a mirror. I say to myself, 'Imagine being stuck with that all my life. I wonder if a beard would improve things.'"

"Oh, Felix, please be serious," I implored him. "This really is a very serious matter."

His smile disappeared and he reached for my hand. "Of course it is. And I'm quite serious when I say that, if you tell the police anything about a mysterious character who you think asked me a lot of suspicious questions about the setup here, I shall simply deny everything. I don't like to make trouble for people. It's the sort of thing that gets one a bad name. And face it, the people who could most easily have taken the silver are Gavin and Rosie. I believe they left the Flints' house about four o'clock, and the murder may have happened as late as that, even if the police think it was a bit earlier. So it's possible, isn't it, that they came straight back here when they left the reception, did the old man in, shoved the silver in their car to create confusion, meaning to dump it somewhere on the way to Exeter, and then took off? And didn't that lawyer say that the first people to be suspected of a murder are the members of the victim's family?"

"You don't believe a word of that," I said. "And what about the search in Hannah's room? Was that just to create further confusion?"

"It might have been. Alternatively, they might have been searching for something they really wanted, something they thought Hannah had. But it's also possible, don't you think, that it was Ledbetter who made that search and was interrupted in the middle of it by our getting back to the house? I like the idea of that. If Ledbetter's been handling Brownlow's financial affairs for him, perhaps for years, and Brownlow got hold of proof that Ledbetter had been swindling him, helping himself out of the funds, mightn't that explain the search as well as the murder?"

"No, it wouldn't, because why was the search in Hannah's room, not in Edward Brownlow's?"

"That's a point. But I can tell you something about Ledbetter that I'm sure of. He's another person who's scared of something. He was lying his head off this evening about his reason for coming here."

"How d'you make that out?"

"He said Brownlow asked him to come here this afternoon to make some change in his will. But don't you remember what Brownlow said on the telephone this morning when Ledbetter rang him up? First Brownlow said something about Haycock, then he said, 'All right, all right, just as you say.' And he sounded annoyed about it and it was then that he said he wasn't going to the reception. So it seems fairly certain that it was Ledbetter who insisted on coming here, though Brownlow wasn't keen about it, and it was Ledbetter who thought the matter was so urgent that it had got to be dealt with today. I haven't any idea what kind of thing it might have been, but I'm sure it had nothing to do with changing a will."

I thought that that made sense. I had just begun to say so when the door opened and Superintendent Hoyle came in.

He had only come to say that he and his men were leaving but that he would be in touch with Miss Brownlow as soon as he had anything significant to tell her and that in any case he would like to see Mr. Gavin Brownlow as soon as he got home. We heard the police cars starting up and driving off and all at once the house felt very empty and silent, almost eerily so, as if, now that the quiet but busy men had gone, ghosts could move in and take possession. Not just the one ghost of the man who was so recently and shockingly dead, but a jostling crowd of others, edging up to us and surrounding us, keeping only just out of sight and whispering of old conflicts and old cruelties that the house must have seen, even if they had been kept secret and hidden over the centuries behind its decorous façade.

"I'd better go upstairs and see how Hannah is," I said.

"And I'll get some supper," Felix said, "though I don't suppose any of us is going to feel very hungry."

We left the room together, Felix going to the kitchen, dodging round the chalk marks left on the floor of the passage that led to it where Edward Brownlow's body had lain, and I up the stairs to Hannah's bedroom.

The room was dark and at first I thought that there was no one there, then I made her out, a shadowy figure sitting in a chair by the window. The curtains were undrawn and faint light came in from a nearly full moon that showed for a moment between hurrying clouds. She was gazing at the blank space of the window and did not turn her head when I came in, but when I switched on the light she said sharply, "Please turn that off."

I did so and advanced a few steps into the dark room.

"The police have gone," I said, "and Felix is getting some supper. Shall I bring it up here to you, or will you come down?"

"I don't want anything," she answered in a toneless voice.

"But I think you ought to have something, even if it's only some hot milk," I said. "I'll bring it up here, shall I?"

"I told you, I don't want anything," she repeated.

I found a chair in the darkness and sat down. "Then perhaps you should go to bed. It's cold in here."

"I never feel the cold. I just want to be left alone."

"I understand that—"

"You don't! No one could understand, unless they'd lost

the only person in the world they've ever cared about. Has that ever happened to you?"

"Not by death, no." I had lost Felix, the Felix whom I had once believed existed, but who had vanished into nothingness under the searching light that intimacy had cast upon him. But at least another Felix was alive and almost as good as new.

"I expect you think I ought to be crying," Hannah went on. "You think it would do me good, don't you? Do you know, I can't cry? And do you know why that is? When I was a child I used to cry very easily—too much, about the most trivial things—and my father couldn't bear it, and one day when I was crying about something unimportant, he sat down facing me and he started to cry too. He was only pretending, of course, but everything I did he imitated. I don't know how long it lasted. It felt like hours. And I've never cried since. As I said, I can't."

"That sounds very cruel," I said.

"Oh, he could be very cruel. But you see, it did me good. My crying was a weakness. He'd no patience with weakness."

"Had he no weaknesses himself?"

"Who hasn't? But I had to be strong. He needed my strength after my mother died. He'd no one else but me."

"He'd Gavin."

"He's useless. My father always knew he couldn't rely on him."

"What will you do now? Will you stay here?"

"Oh no, I couldn't do that. Gavin will be quite ready to sell the house and we'll split what we get for it and I'll buy myself a cottage, probably in Sutherland or even on one of the islands. Somewhere really solitary, where I can go for weeks without seeing anybody. That's what I want, to get away from people. I don't like people and they don't like me. If it hadn't been for my father, I'd have gone away long ago.

I'd the money my mother left me. It isn't much, but I could have managed."

"You seem to have it all thought out."

"Oh, I've had it thought out for a long time. I knew, in the nature of things, that I was bound to be left alone sooner or later, so I thought out very carefully what I should do when it happened."

"Perhaps you'll feel differently when you've got over the worst of the shock and had a little while to think about things."

"No, I shan't."

"Will you keep dogs, or cats, or otters or something?"

"A horse, perhaps."

There was a calm decisiveness in the way she spoke that made me shudder slightly. She really had it all thought out. She might even have been longing for the time to come when she would be free to do what she liked. Perhaps the murderer had done her a favour.

I stood up. "I'm going to bring you some supper, whatever you say. You may find you can eat something when you see it."

I started to feel my way cautiously through the dark room to the door. As I reached it I heard the front doorbell ring again.

In a tone of infinite weariness, Hannah said, "If that's the police, I won't see them. They can't expect it of me."

But it was not the police. By the time that I was halfway down the stairs Felix had emerged from the kitchen, reached the door and opened it. I heard his startled exclamation, "Kay!"

CHAPTER 6

She came in out of the dark, gave Felix a quick kiss, looked up at me and said, "Hello, Virginia."

She was a tall woman with the sort of slender angularity that can confer distinction on the shabbiest of clothes. She was in an old belted raincoat with its collar turned up and had a green silk scarf tied over her dark chestnut hair, but she gave these things a kind of stylishness. She had big, greenish eyes in a face that seemed to be all bone and which, with only a little difference in it, might have been ugly, instead of which it was beautiful. It was pale now, but composed. I had never seen Kay look distraught. An abundance of love affairs, marriage, divorce, and now even murder, she seemed able to take in her stride.

Coming downstairs to meet her, I asked, "Are you alone? Isn't Mr. Haycock with you?"

"No, I wanted to come by myself to talk to Edward," she said, and I realized with a shock that she had not yet heard of the murder. "Paul told me he didn't come in this afternoon because he was scared. Edward got it into his head that Paul was going to marry Hannah and didn't take it too well when he discovered the thing was off. But Edward's always been very good to me, so I thought I ought to come and tell him what I'm going to do. Only I suppose Hannah's told him already . . ." She broke off, only taking it in then that there was something peculiar about the way that Felix and I were looking at her. "What is it?" she asked. "What's the matter?"

Felix answered, "I'm afraid you're too late to talk to Brown-

low, Kay. The poor man met with an unfortunate accident
this afternoon. They've taken him away."

"An accident? D'you mean he's in hospital?" she asked.

"Not exactly," Felix said. "No, not in hospital. In fact, I
rather think he's in the morgue by now."

"For God's sake, Felix!" I exclaimed. "If that's your idea of
breaking things gently, I hope I'm not around when you decide to be blunt. The truth is, Kay, it wasn't an accident at
all. Mr. Brownlow's dead and it was murder. Someone got
into the house and killed him while we were all at the reception after Gavin's wedding. The police left only a little while
ago."

She looked from one to the other of us, checking from our
faces that we meant what we had said. Then she said softly,
"Murder—oh, my God, poor Hannah! Where is she?"

"She's in her room," I said. "I'll go up and tell her you're
here."

"No, wait a minute. Tell me what happened first."

"Come in here then," Felix said, took her arm and led her
into the drawing room. "Of course, nobody knows yet what
really happened. Would you like a drink?"

"Yes, please." She took off her head scarf, shook her hair
loose and unbuttoned her raincoat. Under it she was wearing
a dress of a shimmering dark green, a festive thing which no
doubt she had put on that evening to please her lover. But as
if she felt that it was inappropriate now, she huddled her raincoat round her again. "Go on," she said.

I left it to Felix to tell her the story of the evening, but he
left it to me, and in the end we each told bits of it in turn
while Kay stood with her back to the fire, sipping her drink,
listening attentively, asking no questions.

When the story came a little uncertainly to an end with
Felix and me each waiting for the other to say something
more, she repeated, "Poor Hannah! Shall I go up and see her,
or do you think she'd rather I didn't?"

"I'll go and ask her, shall I?" I said. "She's sitting upstairs in the dark and doesn't seem to want to talk to anyone, but she might be glad to see you."

"It's a funny thing," she said, "but in a way she and I always got on quite well. I think it may have been that she got a kind of vicarious thrill out of my crazy way of living, which she probably thought was even crazier than it ever was."

"Yes," Felix agreed, "it's possible that in her dreams she identified herself with you. Unlikelier things have happened. I've often wondered what kind of dreams go on inside the head of a person like Hannah. I was just getting some supper for us all when you arrived. Have you eaten?"

"Yes, don't bother about me," Kay answered. "I cooked up a meal of sorts in Paul's flat. Go ahead with your own."

"Hannah said she didn't want anything, but perhaps she's changed her mind by now," I said. "I'll go up and see."

But Kay stopped me again. "Just tell me, Virginia, how did she take it when she heard Paul was going to marry me? Paul says she seemed quite pleased."

I thought again of Hannah's shocking, silent laughter as we walked up the drive after Paul had driven off, and observed, "In her way, I believe she was."

Kay gave me a quick look, catching something in my tone that I had not intended her to hear, then said thoughtfully, "It's Gavin, is it? She thinks he'll hate having me around. Damn the woman, I'm quite ready to be sorry for her, but what a mischief-maker she is. Of course, he won't really care in the least. When will he get home, d'you think?"

"If he turns straight back in Exeter, sometime late tonight or in the early morning," I said. "But perhaps they won't come till tomorrow."

"I'm going back to London tomorrow," she said. "We needn't meet. That may be important for Rosie."

Thinking that indeed it might be and hoping that the police would not stop her, I went upstairs to Hannah's room.

It was lighted now and she had changed into pyjamas and a dressing gown.

"Kay's here," I said. "Do you want to see her?"

"Kay? What's she doing here?" she asked.

"She came to see your father. She wanted to talk to him."

"You mean she didn't know he was dead?" She had had one of her astonishing changes of mood. She sounded calm and practical.

"No," I said. "She only came to tell him about her marriage."

"I don't believe it."

"Why not?"

She sat down at her dressing table and started to take the pins out of her hair. As it rolled down over her shoulders she started brushing it languidly.

"I don't know, perhaps it's true," she said. "I suppose the news hasn't travelled far yet."

"It soon will," I said. "I expect the press will be here to-morrow."

"The press?" Her eyes, meeting mine in the mirror, looked blank and horrified. "Oh no, I can't face that! They'll have to go away."

"It isn't always easy to get rid of them when they're after something they want. But perhaps Mr. Ledbetter will handle them for you."

"Stephen? That's a good idea. Yes, I expect he'd do that. Or perhaps you could do it, you and Felix."

"I was going home tomorrow, unless the police told me to stay," I said, "and so was Felix, I think. But if you want us, or one of us, to stay on, it may be possible to arrange it."

"I wish you would." She put down her hairbrush and turned to look at me. "Please—you can't leave me all alone in this great house."

I had never expected to hear from her the appeal that there was in her voice.

"Actually I'd been meaning to ask you about that," I said. "I thought we might be a nuisance here and that, if we were, we could move to a hotel. Gavin will be back tomorrow. You won't be alone anymore. But if you want us to stay, of course we will. Or I will. I can't answer for Felix."

Though I said that, it was my impression that it would be very difficult to pry Felix loose from the place, because he was already showing signs of an absorbing interest in the problem of Edward Brownlow's murder, but I was not going to take responsibility for his actions. It might be that he would recoil from the number of policemen who would be around the house for some days to come and would want to get away from it as soon as he could.

"Thank you," Hannah said. "And, Virginia . . ."

"Yes?"

"You know what I said to you when you were up here before."

"About going to live in a cottage miles away from everywhere?"

"Yes. Please don't say anything about it to the others. I didn't mean it."

"I didn't think you did."

"Really I don't know what I'm going to do."

"Of course you don't. It'll take you some time, after a shock like this, to make up your mind."

"All I feel at the moment is a frightful blankness. But I expect you think I'm a very hysterical person. Repressed and peculiar and all that sort of thing. But I'm not, you know. I'm quite normal."

It was not what I would have called her, but it was natural that she should think it of herself.

"I've yet to meet a normal person," I said. "If one ever came my way, I didn't recognize him. Now what about Kay? Do you want to see her?"

She stood up. "I'll come down." She moved towards the

door. But then she stood still. "You're really sure she didn't know anything about the murder? She just came to talk to Father?"

"It's what she said. Is there any reason it shouldn't be true?"

"I just thought Stephen might have telephoned Paul and told him about it."

"Is he likely to have done that?"

"I'm not sure. They know each other pretty well."

"If he did, why shouldn't Kay have said so?"

"I don't know. But people often have motives for their actions which they won't admit. Queer motives. Things one would never think of."

She gave me a look which for some reason sent a shiver up my spine. I opened the door again and we went downstairs together.

We found Kay and Felix in the kitchen, where Felix had been making sandwiches and more coffee. As Hannah and I came in, Kay went to her and put her arms round her. Hannah remained stiff in the embrace but did not actually shrink from it.

"They've told you everything, I suppose," she said.

"Yes," Kay said, releasing her. "I don't know how to say what I feel."

"It isn't necessary," Hannah said. "All I feel myself at the moment is appallingly tired. I've never felt so tired in my life. I was going to bed when Virginia came in and told me you were here."

"Have a sandwich, Hannah," Felix said, holding out the plateful to her.

She took one automatically, bit into it, then seemed to remember that she did not want anything to eat, looked at it dubiously, then ate it rapidly and reached for another. Felix and I helped ourselves. Kay refused a sandwich but accepted a cup of coffee. We sat down round the table.

"Paul told us you and he are getting married," Hannah said. "Congratulations. I was delighted to hear it."

"Thank you," Kay said.

"It'll be nice, having you living in the neighbourhood." Hannah's tone was brittle and artificial. If she was not remaining in the neighbourhood herself, and I was fairly sure that she would not, even if she did not go to the length of banishing herself to an isolated cottage in the Highlands, Kay's presence in Spellbridge would not make much difference to her. But it sounded as if she was trying to be friendly.

"I'm glad that's how you feel," Kay said. "It's what I wanted to talk over with Edward. Paul didn't think there was any need for it yet and said that you would tell him about it, but I wanted to tell Edward myself, and I'm going back to London tomorrow, so I didn't know when I'd have another chance to do it."

"When did you get to Spellbridge?" Hannah asked. "Have you been here long?"

"I only came this morning," Kay replied. "Paul and I had lunch together, making plans. That's why he got to the reception late, I'm afraid. I kept him talking. It's a rather recent idea of ours, getting married, and we'd quite a lot to talk over. For instance, I don't want to give up my job till we're absolutely sure we're going ahead with it."

"You mean you aren't absolutely sure?" Hannah said in a tone of surprise. "From what Paul said, I thought it was quite definite."

"Well, it is—yes, of course it is. All the same, I'm sort of scared of giving up my job. I've worked all my life. I've never depended on anyone else. It'll feel very strange, having a lot of time on my hands."

"You won't find you have so very much, if you look after your home properly," Hannah said austerely. "That can fill your life, if you're working for someone you care for."

Kay looked doubtful, but plainly thought that this was not the time to argue.

Hannah went on, "I suppose you were the work that Paul said he had waiting at home this afternoon, when he wouldn't come in to tell Father about your engagement himself."

Kay smiled. "I suppose I was. I waited in his flat while he went to the reception."

"The police will ask you about that," Hannah said. "The time he left you, the time he came back, and so on. We've all been asked for our alibis. I haven't got one myself. Of the people they've questioned so far, the only people who have are Felix and Virginia."

Kay looked startled, as if it had not occurred to her till then that she herself could be involved in the murder investigation.

"Yes, I see," she said slowly. "Alibis. Of course. Well, Felix and Virginia told me the police think the murder happened between half past two and half past three. I think I can give Paul an alibi for that time. We had lunch at a pub near his office. I've forgotten its name, but he'll know it. And we stayed there until about half past two, when we went to his flat for a time, till he suddenly remembered the reception and took off in a hurry. That must have been about half past three. So that should clear him."

An ironic gleam in Hannah's eyes showed that she had her own opinion of how the hour in the flat had been spent.

"And you stayed on alone till he got back?" she asked.

"No, as a matter of fact, I went for a walk along the river."

"In the rain?" Felix asked.

Kay gave a laugh, which sounded extraordinarily shocking in that house of trouble.

"Dear Felix, being clever, trying to trip me up," she said. "No, it wasn't raining. It was cold and damp and miserable, but the rain had stopped. I made sure of that before I started out. I think it stopped about the time Paul left. But I only went for a short walk. I didn't walk fifteen miles to Charlwood and another fifteen back. And I came by train this morning, so I hadn't a car. And I didn't take a bus or a taxi. The police will check that, of course, but they'll find I'm telling the truth. And oddly enough, I'd no reason to kill Edward. I'd no reason to fear him, no reason to expect any benefits from him. I just thought of him as someone who'd always been very kind to me."

"Did you know anything about his thinking of leaving you some money in a new will he was going to make?" Hannah asked.

I said quickly, "We don't know that he was. Mr. Ledbetter admitted that was only a guess of his."

"I know," Hannah said. "I was just wondering if Father had said anything to Kay, because if we knew anything about that for certain, it would at least clear up why he wanted to see Stephen so urgently today."

"I haven't seen or heard anything from Edward for nearly a year," Kay replied. "The last time I heard from him was at Christmas, when he sent me a card. He stopped sending me presents when I broke up with Gavin, but he always sent me a Christmas card and I always sent one to him, and that's the only contact I've had with him since the divorce. I can't believe he was going to leave me any money. And suppose he was and I knew it, I'd hardly have killed him before he made the will, should I?" She stood up and laid a hand on Hannah's shoulder. "Hannah dear, you don't seriously think I'm a murderess, do you? I always thought you rather liked me."

Hannah did not reply and her face was expressionless.

Kay began to button her coat. "I think I'd better be going. I've a feeling you half suspect me of having something to do with the murder, even if you don't actually think I committed it. That's disconcerting. I can't say I like it."

She went to the door. Felix got up and followed her out. I

helped myself to another sandwich and, watching Hannah, saw a sardonic little smile appear on her face. As Felix came back into the kitchen, she said, "Of course it's obvious why she really came here this evening, isn't it?"

"Is it?" I said. "What's wrong with the reason she gave us?"

She gave a chuckle which gave me an unpleasant little chill. "She just wanted to find out when the murder was committed so that she could arrange alibis for Paul and herself. But if you ask me, Paul's isn't so good. We've only Kay's word for it that he left his flat at half past three and of course she'd say what he wanted. Hers seems all right if it's true she didn't take a bus or a taxi to get here. If she did, the police will soon find it out."

"But she didn't even know your father was dead when she got here," I said.

"Oh, didn't she!" She repeated her chuckle. "I'm sure Stephen phoned Paul and told him about it. I'm sure he'd do that. But he may not have told him just when the murder was supposed to have happened, so Kay came out here to find out and let us know how utterly impossible it was for her and Paul to have had anything to do with it."

"D'you know, Hannah, I think you may have something," Felix said, taking me by surprise, because I thought she was talking nonsense. "I've been wondering why Kay should take it into her head to come here so late in the evening, just to tell your father about her engagement to Haycock, especially as she knew Hannah would have told him about it already. I thought it was a bit thin."

The telephone rang.

Hannah went to answer it and while she was gone I said to Felix, "Do you really mean what you were implying, that Paul Haycock could have committed the murder?"

"I didn't say that," he pointed out. "All I was coming round to saying was that he and Kay are two frightened people. They must be, to be so anxious to cover their tracks. Like Oliver Flint. And like Ledbetter. And to tell the truth, like me. I just can't believe in that perfect alibi of mine. I feel sure it's going to turn out to have a hole in it."

I shook my head. "My dearest Felix," I said, "I doubt very much if even you can destroy it, however hard you try."

A moment later Hannah reappeared in the doorway.

"That was Gavin," she said. "They're in Exeter. They're coming back in the morning. Now I'm going to bed. I'll see you tomorrow. Good night."

She disappeared again.

Felix and I finished the sandwiches and coffee and did the washing up, then we kissed each other good night and went to bed too.

It was one of the nights when I wished that I had some sleeping pills. Towards the end of my marriage I had got into the habit of taking them, preferring that to lying awake in the unfriendly darkness, wondering what on earth I was to do about the mess that I had made of my life. But some time after our separation I had managed to give them up and now nearly always slept soundly without them. But tonight I was both wide awake and exhausted, which is a very disagreeable condition to be in. Some pills might have been a help.

I thought of having a hot bath, but realizing that the bathroom across the passage was next door to Hannah's room, I thought I might disturb her and abandoned the idea. Instead I looked through the books in the room, found a volume of detective short stories and took it to bed with me. But I did not finish even one story. As soon as I stretched out in the bed my tiredness, like a black cloud, blotted out everything and, with just enough energy left to switch off my bedside lamp, I dumped the book beside it and sank into the stupor of really deep sleep.

I did not open my eyes until nearly eight o'clock next

morning, when, as I did so, I took in the fact that it was day-light and that it was Felix who had wakened me, coming into the room carrying a tray with two cups and a teapot on it. He had never omitted to bring me morning tea all the time that we were married, even after one of our most desperate quar-rels, or perhaps what I should call our bouts of misunder-standing, for we never really quarrelled, and he still made tea for me whenever he stayed with me. Whether or not he trou-bled to get it for himself when he was alone I did not know.

I pushed myself up against my pillows, he put the tray down on my lap and sat down on the edge of the bed. He was in pyjamas and a dressing gown, but he had shaved and combed his hair.

"Have you taken tea to Hannah?" I asked.

"I offered it to her, in fact, I offered to bring her breakfast, but she said she hates having a meal in bed. She's a very difficult woman to do anything for." He reached for the tea-pot and filled the two cups. "I need this myself. I've had hardly any sleep."

"I thought I wasn't going to have any myself," I said, "then I went out like a light. Shock can work that way some-times."

"It wasn't shock that kept me awake," he said. "I was busy. And I found out one or two very interesting things. But I'm not sure if you've woken up enough yet to take them in. Drink some tea, then I'll tell you about them."

He brought cigarettes out of the pocket of his dressing gown, lit one, picked up his cup of tea and drank.

"It's all right, I'm wide awake," I said, which I had not been a moment before, but what he had said had brought that state about very rapidly. "What have you been getting up to?"

"Doing a little quiet investigating, that's all," he said. "I thought I might not have another chance. Probably the po-

MYNDERSE LIBRARY
31 Fall Street
Seneca Falls, New York 13148

lice will get down to searching the place more thoroughly today, and anyway, Rosie and Gavin will be here."

"The Flints want them to stay with them," I said. "Nora doesn't like the idea of Rosie staying in a house where there's been a murder."

"Rosie may have other ideas. Not to mention Gavin. But I felt fairly sure no one would interfere with me if I went straight ahead and did what I wanted. I didn't think Hannah would come down from her room again, and if you heard me prowling around and came down to see who it was, I could have got you to help me."

"Why didn't you do that anyway?"

"I thought you were probably very tired and needed your sleep."

"And you didn't think I'd help you, you thought I'd try to stop you, as of course I should have. We're only visitors here. This murder has nothing to do with us. We've no right to go searching through the Brownlows' things." I drank some tea. "What did you find out?"

He gave me his sly grin. "I knew you'd be interested. I'll explain in a moment, but tell me first, what do you know about Hannah's finances?"

"Nothing to speak of," I said. "I know she and Gavin each inherited a certain amount from their mother, but I've no idea how much. It's what Gavin was living on, together with what Kay was earning, while he was trying to get started in London and they never seemed exactly affluent, did they? And since then inflation will have made it worth even less. Why?"

"It's just that, when I was going through that bureau in Hannah's room to see if I could get a hint of what the murderer might have been looking for, I came on her bank statements and cancelled cheques. The bureau was very easy to search, she keeps everything so tidy, and there the bank statements were in a folder, with cheques for the last two years in an envelope under it. And as far as I could make out, her income is about four thousand a year and comes to her in a lot of driblets from various investments, all good conservative things like building societies and so on, and up to about eighteen months ago her withdrawals were about what you'd expect, something like a hundred pounds a month to self, sometimes a bit more, sometimes a bit less, which I suppose was for casual spending, and odd amounts to local shops, not a great deal, perhaps for clothes, and a fair amount for income tax, which came high, because it was all unearned. She doesn't seem to have contributed to the household expenses or spent anything to speak of on holidays, and she lived just about comfortably within her income. Then all of a sudden those monthly cheques to self jumped from a hundred to five hundred."

"Wait a minute," I said. "Five hundred a month would add up to six thousand a year."

"Just what I was coming to."

"Where was the extra amount coming from? Did she run a big overdraft?"

"No, she was realizing capital. The bank seems to have kept her share certificates for her and there's a letter from the manager, very gently advising her against what she was doing, but she seems to have gone ahead with it."

I thought it over. "That doesn't sound like Hannah."

"That's what I thought myself. And naturally I wondered what she'd been doing with the money."

"And being you, I know what conclusion you came to," I said. "You decided she was paying blackmail."

He gave me a thoughtful look. "You don't think that's possible."

"Well, does it sound like Hannah? Can you see her ever doing anything that would give anyone a hold on her that would make her part with five hundred a month?"

"I can, as a matter of fact. She's unbalanced enough to

have done some pretty strange things in her time. But just when I was thinking about that, I made another very curious discovery. Last April she stopped those withdrawals of five hundred and started paying five hundred *into* her account."

Anything to do with money always confuses me as soon as it becomes more complicated than receiving my salary cheque and paying my bills.

"Doesn't it mean she made some investment that had started to pay off, or something like that?" I said.

"I wondered about that, and I think in a sense it might be possible," Felix said. "But I'm puzzled by it. I've had just one idea. April, I thought—why April? Is there anything significant about the date? And it struck me then, one or two other things happened in April. Can't you think what they were?"

"It's about when Gavin and Rosie got engaged, isn't it? But what could that have to do with it?"

"Nothing, probably, though you never know. But it's also when Nora Flint inherited a lot of money from a grandaunt."

"I believe it was. But again, what could that have to do with the thing you found out?"

"Well, I've been wondering if it's possible—I'd like to know what you think—that Hannah had been helping the Flints out for about a year and then when they came into the grandaunt's money they started to pay her back. How about that?"

"You think she's generous enough to have done that?"

"I don't know, but it might not have been plain generosity. We were talking about her having made some investment that had started to pay off. Suppose that's what it was, a loan to the Flints, secured by their expectations from the grandaunt, which will be paid off with interest by degrees."

"I don't think that sounds like Hannah either," I said. "Not if it meant realizing capital to do it. She's the kind of person who'd far sooner have the small, safe income that she's always had and that she's never had to think about, than take any risks. I think generosity's more probable than that. But why to the Flints? She seems to like Nora fairly well, but she doesn't like Oliver at all and his attitude to her doesn't suggest he feels indebted to her. Still, I can think of someone else whom she might have helped."

"Who?"

"Her father."

Felix shook his head. "If a man like Brownlow gets into a jam for money, a sum like five hundred a month wouldn't have gone far to help him. It would have had to be thousands. All the same, I did think of that myself and to make sure about it I investigated some accounts of his that I found in Hannah's bureau. There were his bank statements and the passbook of his deposit account and his cancelled cheques and old cheque books with the stubs all neatly filled in in Hannah's writing. She seems to have acted as his secretary as well as his housekeeper. All the cheques for the household accounts were filled in by her and just signed by him. And there was always a surplus of much more than five hundred in his current account, not to mention several thousands in the deposit account, so he certainly wasn't in difficulties. Not in his private affairs, at least. And if the firm was in difficulties, as I said, what Hannah was paying simply wouldn't have been enough to signify."

"You seem to have had a busy night," I said. "Did you find out anything else?"

He gave a great yawn. "Isn't that enough?"

"I don't see that any of it has anything to do with the murder of Hannah's father."

"I didn't say it had, but it's interesting, all the same. God, I'm tired. I only had about two hours' sleep. And then I dreamt about Kay, which was delightful, but not restful. You know, I could easily fall in love with her again. There's a sort of exaggeration in her looks, all those wonderful bones with hardly anything covering them, something only just this side of the grotesque, that you find in most really beautiful people. Damn that man Haycock. Why did he suddenly have to come on the scene? She likes me too, I can feel that."

"Then do something about it, don't just talk," I said. "But I was thinking, mightn't Hannah have been lending money to somebody else, not the Flints or her father? That they started paying her back in April, when the Flints inherited their money, could easily have been coincidence."

"Are you thinking of Gavin?"

"No, I doubt very much if she'd help Gavin out, whatever difficulties he got into."

"Even if family pride was somehow involved?"

"Perhaps that just might make her do it. But speaking of Gavin, something's just occurred to me. She's convinced he only married Rosie for her money. In fact, she seems rather to feel that nobody ever does anything except for money."

"She may not be entirely right, but she may not be as far out as you seem to think," Felix said. "I get obsessed by it myself from time to time."

"Only when you're very short of it. I don't think she's ever gone short."

He gave a perplexed frown. "But what about it? Is that important?"

"I don't know," I said. "It's just something I thought of."

Felix stood up and lifted the tray from my lap. "I suppose it's the sort of thing that could mean she's never been loved, or hasn't loved anyone else, which is sad, but like all the other things we've found out about her, I don't see what it can have to do with the murder. One thing I'm sure of is that she's a very unhappy woman, and that could mean a dangerous one, don't you think? Well, see you at breakfast."

He went out.

It was only after he had gone that I realized that I had not asked him if he was going to tell Mr. Hoyle about the discoveries that he had made in the night. Feeling about the police as he did, he almost certainly would not. In that case, ought I to do so? I could not make up my mind. Deciding to have a bath, I got out of bed, put on my dressing gown and slippers and wandered off to the bathroom.

CHAPTER 7

The press, in the persons of three local reporters, arrived about nine o'clock. Felix supplied them with a fluent if not very accurate account of what had happened and did not let them approach Hannah.

Rosie and Gavin did not arrive until nearly twelve o'clock. On their way they had stopped at the police station in Spellbridge and been kept there for some time, and by the time that they reached Charlwood they knew as much about the murder as Hannah, Felix or I. But Gavin was not altogether prepared to believe this. He wanted a firsthand account from each of us of what we had seen and what we had told the police.

Felix, who had just returned from a session in the photographic studio of Oliver Flint, told a far more coherent story of what had happened than Hannah or I, though naturally he said nothing about his nocturnal rambling about the house. In a few minutes that he and I had to ourselves in the drawing room while Rosie and Gavin were upstairs in his room, unpacking their suitcases, and Hannah was in the kitchen, I asked him if he had found it worth his while, being photographed. He shrugged his shoulders.

"I didn't find out anything I didn't know already," he said. "But he's good, very good. Better than I expected. If he weren't bone lazy, I think he could have become famous."

I had often had the same feeling about Felix himself. With his imagination and intelligence, I believed that he might have achieved almost anything, if only he had been capable of occasional hard work.

"What did you expect to find out?" I asked.

"Nothing special," he said. "But there was one thing that was interesting in its way. A photograph of Hannah that he had up on the wall. I don't wonder she doesn't like him."

"What was wrong with it?"

"Only that it made her utterly frightening. A sort of gorgon. You could almost see the snakes writhing in her hair. When he saw me looking at it, he laughed and said it was one of the best things he'd ever done, but that it had cost him her friendship. There was another photograph that took my fancy, a family group of himself and Nora and Rosie, as different from the one of Hannah as it could possibly be. It was really charming."

"If he was in it himself, I wonder who took it."

"Hannah, perhaps, while they were still friends."

I was just about to say that I did not feel sure that they had ever been friends, that friendship was not one of Hannah's talents, when she came in, saying coldly that she had not expected to have to provide lunch for five people that day and that we should have to be satisfied with tinned ham, salad and cheese.

"I hardly eat anything for lunch myself when I'm alone," she said. "Just some yogurt and an apple. I do all my cooking in the evening. But I expect you're all hungry and want drinks as well."

She made it sound extremely unreasonable of us.

Gavin, coming in with Rosie, heard her and said, "Drinks? Yes. But I can't say I'm hungry. Rosie, what about you?"

"You'll think it's awful if I say I'm terribly hungry," Rosie answered, "but breakfast seems hours ago."

"Youth," Gavin said. "She eats all the time. It's extraordinary, isn't it, that she can do it and keep that lovely figure? I've warned her she'll have to slow up as she gets older." He sounded more absorbed in Rosie than in the death of his father, but as he poured out drinks he went on, "I wish to God we'd made the old man come to the reception with us yesterday, even if he wasn't feeling well. If we had, he'd be alive today. I feel now as if it was my fault that we didn't at least try."

"It's a little late to blame yourself for that now," Hannah said. "The time for it was when you saw how Stephen's telephone call upset him."

"You saw that yourself," Gavin said, "but you left him alone here and went to the reception."

"I offered to stay, but he told me to go," Hannah said. "He wanted to be alone to talk to Stephen."

"Then he wouldn't have wanted me to stay either, would he?"

"I'm not sure he wouldn't have been glad if you had. After all, you know far more about his affairs than I do. You might have been a help."

Gavin flushed suddenly and looked extremely angry. "And just how could I have stayed? Rosie might have had something to say on the matter."

"You never really cared for him," Hannah said. "Other things always came first."

"Oddly enough, my marriage did come first."

I did not understand what was happening, except that this was one of the sort of quarrels that they must have been in the habit of having for most of their lives. It seemed amazingly pointless. How was Gavin to guess that his father was going to be murdered while we were all at the reception?

I said, "Rosie, Nora told me to tell you and Gavin that you should go to stay with them if you wanted to. I'm sorry, I ought to have told you as soon as you got here, before you unpacked, in case it's what you want to do."

She looked uncertainly from Gavin to Hannah, then back at Gavin.

"I don't know . . ." she said hesitantly, then left the sentence hanging, unsure of herself, wanting to do whatever he preferred.

"There's something else you don't know," Hannah said quickly, as if this was something she wanted to say before the two of them perhaps escaped her. "Kay was here last night and I had a talk with Paul after the reception. Can you believe it, the two of them are getting married?"

"Kay?" Gavin exclaimed, incredulous and deeply startled. "To Paul? *Paul?*" He looked stunned. "I don't believe you!"

"Oh yes, it's true," Hannah said and laughed almost gaily. "Ask Felix and Virginia."

He went on staring at her. "But that's impossible."

"Why?"

"It just is. Impossible. It can't be."

"Both Kay and Paul will tell you it's going to be. And it's hardly for you to object, is it? Of course, Kay will be coming to live in Spellbridge and you'll probably be running into one another and she was worried that you might not like that. But you'll just have to get used to it, won't you? Look how beautifully Felix and Virginia manage."

He made an impatient gesture. "It isn't that. It's the thought of her marrying *Paul* . . ." He hit his forehead with his knuckles. "What the hell am I going to do about it?"

"Just why have you got to do anything about it?" Rosie asked. She sounded merely curious, but it struck me that she had become noticeably paler during the last moments.

"I can't help feeling responsible for her still, that's all," he answered. "She could have married half a dozen other people —I wished she would—and then she has to go and choose Paul."

"What's wrong with Paul? I thought you were friends." Rosie's voice was as level as before, but with a new note in it that disturbed me.

"So we are, in a way, or used to be," Gavin replied.

"Then why aren't you pleased about it?"

"Because . . . Oh hell, I can't let it happen. I'll have to do something about it."

"It seems to me you're the last person who ought to try to do anything about it." A biting note was now distinct in Rosie's voice. "Isn't it simply that you can't bear the thought of Kay marrying anyone at all? You may as well tell me the truth. The sooner I know, the better. I believe I've always known it in the back of my mind. You're still in love with her, aren't you?"

He gave her a dazed look, as if he found it difficult to drag his mind back to what she was saying from wherever it had strayed.

"In love with Kay—me?" he said.

"Yes, yes, yes!" she suddenly shouted at him. "In love with dear, bloody Kay, as you always have been. You've never got her out of your system. I tell you, I've always known it, though, like a fool, I shut my eyes to it. She's beautiful and she's clever and she could always wind you round her little finger. And I know it took some shoving from my mother to make you think of marrying me. It was she who put it into your mind, wasn't it?"

He thrust his fingers through his grey hair. "She only said she thought the age difference didn't matter. She said she was sure—well, that you cared for me."

"And you thought I might be able to cure you of going on wanting Kay forever and ever when you couldn't have her."

"Damn it, I didn't want her! I was glad to get rid of her!"

"Then why can't you bear her marrying Paul?"

"That's something quite different."

"Oh, I'm sure you believe it's something quite different. I'm sure you've convinced yourself your motives are absolutely disinterested. But I don't think you've convinced anyone else. You haven't convinced me. I'm only thankful it's come out now before we'd time to build up anything together which it would have been unbearable to bring crashing down. I can just write it off as experience, can't I? I'll know better next time." Her pallor had changed to a hectic flush. Her voice was shaking and she was very near tears, but too angry to let them pour down. "I'm going home now. Don't come after me. You can send my case on later and we can talk it all over some other time. Just at the minute I couldn't face it."

She went swiftly to the door.

I wanted to tell Gavin to stop being a fool, to take her in his arms and kiss her hard and refuse to listen to her if she argued. But there was something about him that checked me. He looked shocked and bewildered, but there was something more than that. As Rosie slammed the door behind her I realized what it was. He looked scared. Like Oliver Flint, like Stephen Ledbetter, like Paul Haycock, as Felix had pointed out.

Gavin took a few uncertain steps towards the door, as if he meant to follow Rosie, but Felix said, "Why not give her a little time to cool down? Poor girl, she's tired and she's hungry. Let her mother feed her and give her some good advice. She'll probably be back soon in a different state of mind."

"It's an extraordinary thing," Gavin muttered in a puzzled tone, "but she's been so utterly rational ever since we got Stephen's message in the hotel. She said it didn't matter, the honeymoon being off, that what had happened was far too serious for us to think about ourselves, and she wanted us to drive back straight away. It was I who said we could leave early in the morning instead. Then it was her idea that we should go to the police station on our way here, as she said they were certain to want to talk to me. Then after all that she flies into this astounding rage because I say something about not liking the idea of Kay marrying Paul."

"You said rather a lot," I said. "You seemed rather excited about it."

"But who'd have dreamt she had all that jealousy bottled

up inside her?" He poured out a second drink for himself, too absorbed in his problem to look round and see if anyone else wanted one too. "She said she'd known all along I was still in love with Kay. And that's utterly untrue. I got over Kay a long time ago. The one thing Rosie said which I suppose is true is that it's a good thing this has come out into the open now. If she's really so fantastically jealous, I'll have to try and deal with it somehow."

"Of course, you could always tell her the real reason why you don't want Kay to marry Paul," Hannah said.

It was a simple enough thing to say, yet it had the effect that Hannah's remarks so often had of dragging a sudden silence after them.

Then Gavin said with a viciousness which I had never heard in his voice before, "It's your doing, isn't it?"

She seemed oddly pleased by the accusation, but she said coolly, "Making her flare up like that? How could I possibly know she would?"

"But you knew what I'd feel about that marriage," he said. "You could have told me about it in private, couldn't you?"

"And help you to deceive your wife right from the start? Really, I'm not that kind of person."

"You could have given me time to think out what we ought to do."

"*We?*" she said. "Are you expecting me to do anything about it?"

"Yes, Hannah, I am," he said harshly.

"I don't intend to do anything."

"You will, I think. If not for Kay's sake, then for Father's."

"He's dead," she answered. "Nothing we do can help him or hurt him."

"What a cold-blooded bitch you are," he said. "I wonder if that great love you were supposed to have had for him had any reality, or was it a kind of hate?"

"People much more experienced than I am have said that

the two things can often be very alike," she said serenely. "Now I'm going to get lunch. It won't be anything much, but I didn't have much warning, did I?"

"I don't want any lunch," Gavin said explosively. "I'm going to a pub in Spellbridge. I can't stay in this house any longer. I may do you an injury if I stay."

He strode out of the room.

"Quite like when we were children," Hannah remarked. "We had fearful fights then. He's got a terrible temper, you know. Perhaps you've never seen it before. And I'm told I once threw a knife at him. I don't remember doing it, but one often blots out that sort of memory, doesn't one? Well, I'll have lunch ready in a few minutes."

She left the room too.

Felix lit a cigarette. "Just at the moment I'm feeling thankful I was an only child," he said. "Talk of blood being thicker than water! In this family, it seems to me, it's a good deal thinner."

I had been an only child myself and had deeply envied those of my friends who had had brothers and sisters, but I have to admit that I have never seen any evidence that such people turn out either better or worse in the end than only children.

"I wish I understood what all that was about," I said. "I couldn't make any sense of it."

"No, but there's something they know which they're covering up, something to do with their father, whether or not it's got anything to do with the murder," Felix said.

"Why do you think Gavin is so appalled at the thought of Kay's marriage?" I asked. "Can Rosie have been right? Is he still in love with her?"

"I doubt it, but it isn't impossible. Rosie may have felt there was something lacking in her relationship with him and that's how she explained it. We don't know much about it, do we?"

"It seemed to me that what he was upset about wasn't that Kay was getting married, but that it was Paul Haycock she was marrying."

"Yes, that was fairly clear, but it was when he dragged his father into it that things between him and Hannah got really raw."

"I find Paul Haycock an enigmatic figure," I said. "He and Hannah are supposed to have been on the edge of getting engaged, then suddenly it's off and he's getting married to Kay and Hannah seems quite pleased about it. And Gavin says he and Paul are friends in a way, but implies pretty plainly that they aren't really, and then he gets into this awful state at the thought of his marrying Kay. It looks as if he knows something very discreditable about him. It's all rather odd, isn't it?"

"What did you make of Haycock yourself when you met him yesterday?" Felix asked.

"Nothing special. I thought he was just ordinary."

"But you've never been strong on intuition. Now my impression of him was that he was one big bluff, not an ordinary man at all, but someone who works at making you think that's what he is."

"That's just hindsight, because of the slightly queer turn things have taken today."

"No, I assure you, I felt it at once. And I've been worrying myself at the thought of Kay marrying him. She's worth something better."

"Well, perhaps she's seen under the surface and found it's more exciting than one would think." I smiled at him a little unkindly. "You've really got Kay on your mind, haven't you?"

"Do you blame me?"

"I haven't blamed you for anything for years," I said. "I always found it wearing and pointless. Anyway, in this case I'm not likely to. She's got great attractions, I've always seen that."

"God help me, I believe you're jealous for once," Felix said.

"Not at all—"

As I spoke the door opened and Gavin reappeared.

He went straight to the drinks tray and poured himself out another whisky. I thought that he seemed to be drinking a good deal more than I remembered him ever doing in the old days.

"I thought you were going into Spellbridge," Felix said.

"I was just leaving when I saw the police coming," Gavin answered. "I thought they might want to talk to me again, so I turned back. There they are."

The front doorbell had just rung. He gave a deep sigh, as if out of sudden, unbearable weariness, put down his glass and turned towards the door. But before he reached it we heard Hannah cross the hall. There were voices there, then Hannah appeared in the drawing-room doorway, followed by Superintendent Hoyle and Sergeant Gresham.

"Good morning," the superintendent said heartily to us all. "I've some news which I think may be of interest to you. I can't say we're ready to bring a charge for the murder of Mr. Brownlow, but we've made a discovery which I think is of great significance."

Hannah invited the two detectives to sit down and we all arranged ourselves about the room on the stiff, damask-covered chairs.

Mr. Hoyle went on, "We've got the man who stole the silver. As soon as we knew silver was missing we put out a call for him, as we know it's his line, and he was picked up this morning, trying to deliver it to his usual fence, a man with an antique shop in Spellbridge. But he'd heard about the murder on the grapevine and didn't want to get involved, so he got his wife to call us while he kept our friend Pietro Bruno talking."

"Pietro Bruno?" Felix said. "An Italian?"

The superintendent looked at him. "Does the name mean anything to you?"

"Oh no," Felix answered expressionlessly. "I just thought it an odd sort of name to hear in Spellbridge."

"Almost certainly not his real one," Mr. Hoyle said. "We rather think it's Brown. Anyway, we collected the stuff and it's at the police station now, along with the man himself. And he kept talking so fast you might think he was afraid we were going to interrupt him, only not about the murder. He admits he knew about the valuable silver in this house and about the reception and that he thought the house would be empty. He claims that he drove here openly about half past two, saw Miss Brownlow leave, drove up to it, ready with some story about selling encyclopaedias if it should turn out after all that there was still someone in the house, got no answer, got ready to break in, then thought of trying the door first, found it wasn't locked and walked in. So far so good. We may be able to check that if we can find anyone who saw the car either in front of the house or on the way here. But after that his story gets a little less credible."

He moved his sturdy bulk about on the small, hard chair, trying to find some way of accommodating himself more comfortably.

"Half past two," he repeated. "And he swears he saw no body. But if Mr. Brownlow was still alive then, wouldn't he have answered the door when Bruno rang? Perhaps not. Perhaps he was upstairs asleep and didn't hear the bell. But whatever the facts are, Bruno says he never went down the passage to the kitchen. He'd found all the silver he was expecting in this room and the dining room and made off with it without troubling to search the house for more. And that's just possibly true. I mean, it isn't actually impossible, even if we're not inclined to believe it. For the fact is, if he didn't go down the passage, he wouldn't have seen Mr. Brownlow's body, if it had been there, because you can't see along the passage from the hall. So it doesn't help us much to determine the time of the murder."

"But doesn't it mean you were right yesterday when you said two people could have come into the house?" I said. "The thing you said wouldn't be such a tremendous coincidence."

"Ah, because the silver wasn't taken just to mislead us, as we were inclined to believe," he said. "It was simply a straightforward job by a known thief."

"Yes," I said. "And besides him, someone came into the house and searched for something that wasn't silver. Can't Mr. Bruno tell you anything about it?"

He rubbed a hand down one side of his large, ruddy face.

"I think he could, if he would, you know," he said. "It's only an impression, but I believe he saw the body. It could be one of the reasons why he tried to get rid of the silver so quickly, though that turned out to be a mistake. But it happens that this Bruno is a very sophisticated sort of thief. He's very intelligent, quite well educated, actually went to a university once, though he didn't stick it out long enough to get a degree. I think he'd be capable of making that very noticeable search through Miss Brownlow's papers just to make us think what we did, that the theft of the silver was the blind and the murder was done by someone who had some fairly close connection with the Brownlow family."

"But you don't think he's the murderer, do you?" Felix said.

"Well, he could be," the superintendent answered. "If Mr. Brownlow was asleep when Bruno rang the bell and came into the house and was only disturbed later by some noise downstairs, he might have come down and interrupted him just as he was taking a look into Miss Brownlow's room to see if there was anything of value in it. I don't like his story about not troubling to look there. And he could have lost his head then, snatched up the poker and knocked Mr. Brownlow out. Quite likely he didn't mean to kill him. We've never known him go in for violence before. But there's always a first time for anything. Then, seeing what he'd done, he could have had the ingenious idea of pulling open drawers and scattering papers about for the reason we've just been into. He's a crafty fellow. I wouldn't put it past him."

"But he may not have faked that search at all," I said. "Hannah, suppose the search was genuine, haven't you any idea what he might have been searching for?"

She gave me a considering look, her eyes narrowed, and I felt that for a moment she was on the edge of telling us something. But then she gave a slow shake of her head.

"I'd absolutely nothing in there worth taking," she said.

"Now that brings me to a matter I was going to raise," the superintendent said. "What about other places in the house? Before we get too attached to the idea that we've caught our murderer, I'd like you to tell me if you know of anything, anything at all, some letters, for instance, or other papers, that might have been in Mr. Brownlow's possession and which someone—the murderer, if he isn't Bruno—thought were a danger to him and thought he'd be able to get hold of at a time when he believed the house was empty. Please think, Miss Brownlow. Think very carefully. He may have made a mistake by beginning searching in your room, but couldn't there be something somewhere else which he never got around to because he was caught by Mr. Brownlow, lost his head after he'd killed him, panicked and bolted?"

Hannah again shook her head.

"I can't think of anything," she said.

He went on, "You see, if the murderer didn't get around to finding it, it'll still be there and may give us an invaluable clue to his identity."

"But you've got your murderer," Gavin said sharply. "Isn't it obvious it's this man Bruno?"

"Pretty obvious," Mr. Hoyle agreed placidly. "But I'm never very fond of jumping to conclusions. Where did your father keep most of his papers, Mr. Brownlow?"

"In his office, naturally," Gavin replied. "Household accounts and so on were kept in my sister's room."

"But hadn't he anywhere of his own here where he'd write private letters and things of that kind?"

It seemed to me that both the Brownlows were extraordinarily unwilling to answer.

It must have seemed so too to Mr. Hoyle, for he said quietly, "I can get a search warrant, you know, if you aren't willing to cooperate, and take the whole house to pieces. It may be important."

The brother and sister exchanged glances, then Hannah shrugged her shoulders.

"My father had a small room next to his bedroom which he used as a sort of study," she said. "He'd bring work home sometimes and sit up there and sometimes he'd just sit and read, when he felt like being alone. I don't know what papers he kept in it. But I think I can show you something that may interest you without your having to turn the place upside down. When you see it, you'll understand why my brother and I didn't want to say anything to you about it. I suppose I ought to say I'm sorry we didn't, but I'd hoped for the sake of our father's name that we shouldn't have to. If you'll come with me, I'll show you."

"Hannah, for God's sake—" Gavin burst out, then stopped himself and started cursing quietly.

She had started towards the door and he followed her, motioning to the two detectives to precede him. I heard them cross the hall and mount the stairs. I saw a look of avid curiosity on Felix's face. He would have loved to follow them, but as a mere guest in the house it would have been difficult for him to find a good excuse for doing so when he had not been invited. He went to one of the tall windows and stood gazing out, his slim body tense with frustration.

I went and stood beside him, also gazing out. After the dreary rain of the day before, it was bright and fine, with a clear blue sky and sunshine pouring in at the window onto our faces. If there had not been so many dead leaves scattered over the lawn and the beech trees near the house had not shown so many bare twigs through the leaves that still clung to them, it could almost have been taken for a summer's day.

"So you did talk a little too freely to your friend Bruno," I said.

"I always call him Pete," Felix answered.

"Why does he want to be taken for an Italian?"

"I think he feels that in the circles he moves in it gives him status. He comes from Liverpool."

"He's in serious trouble."

"The bloody fool."

"What do you think, did he do the murder?"

"Oh no, I told you, he's a professional. If he wanted to knock Brownlow out, he'd have left him comfortably unconscious, he wouldn't have killed him."

"Anyone can make a mistake. As Mr. Hoyle said, there's always a first time."

"Look," Felix said, turning on me with a fierceness that was not at all characteristic of him, "he is not a murderer! And crafty fellow though he may be, he hasn't got it in him to think of a subtle little dodge like faking a search in Hannah's room to make it look as if the murder was an inside job. Remember, the theory is that he'd come peaceably into an empty house to do a little quiet stealing, and he'd just stumbled over a murdered corpse or done the murder himself. And there was his car outside the house where anyone could see it. Naturally, I don't suppose it was his own car, it was just one he'd picked up for the job, but wouldn't his instinct have been to get away from the place as soon as he could? Of course it would. And you're forgetting there's something upstairs that Hannah and Gavin have been keeping very quiet about which may throw an altogether new light on the scene. And Gavin was very angry with Hannah for giving in to police pressure and admitting the thing was there at all. I wish I knew what it was."

"It's got something to do with that quarrel they were having just before the police arrived," I said. "That was something to do with their father."

"That's probable. But I'll tell you something, I'm going to stick around till Pete's out of trouble—as far as the murder's concerned, that's to say. I can't help the fool if he got himself caught with the silver, but I'll stick around unless they actually push me out until he's cleared of the killing. I'm certain he didn't do it, just as I'm certain he didn't fake that search in Hannah's room, though, d'you know, that's given me an idea. Rather an interesting idea . . ." His gaze became abstracted.

It is one of Felix's more attractive qualities that he is extremely loyal to his friends—if it is attractive, that is to say, to be loyal to such people as professional burglars just because you and they happen to have met often enough in a variety of pubs to have formed casually comfortable and trustful relationships. But at the moment I was not sure whether Felix's sudden decision to stay on in the Brownlows' house was motivated by that loyalty or by simple curiosity.

One of the daydreams with which he sometimes entertains himself is that he is a great detective and I thought that this fantasy might already have him in its grip. If it had, he was liable to become very quiet and secretive, waiting for some dramatic moment to reveal the depth of his penetration. Of course, I was feeling very curious myself and turned away eagerly from the window when I heard footsteps on the stairs once more and waited for the door to open.

When it did only Hannah and Gavin came in. The two detectives had left. Gavin came in quickly, picked up his unfinished drink and drained it.

"Now you've done it!" he said furiously to Hannah. "I hope you're satisfied."

"What else could I do?" she responded.

"You could have made a fuss and insisted on them getting a search warrant. That would have given us a little time. I was meaning to destroy the letters the moment I got a chance. As it was, you led them straight to them."

I was beginning to understand what Hannah and also Paul Haycock had meant when they spoke of the violent emotions that seethed behind Gavin's quiet exterior. He was in a rage now. The hand holding his glass was trembling.

"If I hadn't, they'd only have turned the place upside down," Hannah replied calmly, "and I'd have had to tidy up. At least I've spared myself that."

"At the cost of what's going to turn out a first-class scandal," Gavin said. "Are you going to enjoy that?"

"I'd sooner it hadn't happened. Now I'm going to get lunch and you can stay for it or go to your pub in Spellbridge, just as you like."

She went out.

Gavin flung himself down in a chair. He was looking more distraught than angry now and, examining the glass in his hand, seemed to be wondering whether or not to have another drink. But deciding against it, he put the glass down on a table near him.

"I suppose all this is very mysterious to you," he muttered glumly.

"A little," Felix answered. "But don't feel there's any need to tell us anything. It's nothing to do with us."

That was a polite formula. He could hardly contain his curiosity.

"Oh, it's certain to come out now," Gavin said, "so I may

as well explain it. You see, my highly respected father was a crook. He has been for years, though I only found out about it after I came to work in the firm. He practised bribery. That's crooked, isn't it? And the man who took the bribes was Paul Haycock. He's on the Housing and Development Committee in Spellbridge and ever since he became chairman he's been steering contracts our way. That block of flats that are going up near here, it was his doing we got the permit to build them. There was a lot of opposition to it, but he squashed it. I don't know the details of how much he got out of us. My father didn't really want me to know anything about it. He knew I'd be against it. It was by chance I got onto what was happening, opening a letter to him from Paul, sent to him here, not to the office, which I thought was addressed to me and which was thanking him for his most generous present. That started me asking questions and my father admitted there'd been a number of those presents and that they'd meant thousands to the firm. I was still pretty naïve in business matters in those days and I was appallingly shocked. If I'd thought of bribing anyone, I shouldn't have dreamt of going above a few good lunches and a case of whisky at Christmas. I tried to persuade my father to drop the whole thing, but he only laughed at me. So I gave up and accepted things. I might have got out if I'd been tougher than I am, but I'd already failed once trying to get started on my own, and I was wanting to get married. So that makes me a crook too, doesn't it, and explains why I seem to need rather a lot of whisky? And now Hannah's put the evidence in the hands of the police and the whole thing's going to be blown open and my father's reputation will be shot to bits and I may find I'm in quite deep trouble myself."

"Pretty reckless of Haycock, wasn't it, putting anything in writing?" Felix said.

"I think Father insisted on some sort of receipt," Gavin answered. "He wanted some hold on Paul in case he didn't come through with what he'd been paid for, or had a rush of conscience to the head. Not that he need have worried about Paul's conscience. Ever since he got onto the council he was just asking to be corrupted. According to my father, it was Paul who started dropping hints to him, suggesting they might come to some arrangement."

I began to understand now why Hannah had said on the walk up the drive after the reception that Paul Haycock had every reason to be afraid of Gavin and why the thought of this had made her shake with laughter. Paul Haycock could never have been sure how far he could trust Gavin.

I said, "And that's the real reason why you were so upset when you heard he was going to marry Kay. You've still enough feeling for her that you hated the idea of her marrying someone as crooked as that."

Gavin gave me a blank look, as if he did not mean to answer me, but then he nodded.

"But I couldn't explain that to Rosie, could I, without dragging this whole beastly business into the open?" he said. "I was still hoping I could cover it up in some way."

"But it gives Paul Haycock a pretty strong motive for murder," I said. "If your father told him you knew about what was going on and that he didn't feel he could count on you to keep quiet about it, mightn't he have felt he had to get those letters back at any price? Without them, I suppose you'd have had no solid evidence against him. So mightn't he have come to the house when he thought it would be empty and searched for them and been surprised by your father and had some sort of quarrel with him and killed him? Hunting in Hannah's room instead of your father's might have been because he knew enough of the ways of the household to believe all important papers were kept there. And he hasn't really got an alibi. Kay says he left her about half past three, but she may not be telling the truth. She may just be saying that to cover him."

"Do you think Kay knows about this bribery?" Felix asked. "Would she worry about it?"

Hannah answered from the doorway, "She'll only worry now that the payments will stop. And of course Paul will have to resign his position on the council and, for all we know, will go to gaol for a bit. I shouldn't be surprised if we hear soon the marriage is off."

Understanding dawned on Gavin's face. "So that's why you handed those letters over to the police so willingly. Revenge on Paul for what he did to you. You've just been waiting for an opportunity like this, haven't you? And you pretended you didn't really care."

"I didn't." She smiled in a way that made me think of Felix's description of the photograph of her that he had seen in Oliver Flint's studio. Felix had said that it had been the face of a gorgon, that you could almost see the snakes writhing in her hair. "Come to lunch. Tinned ham, salad and cheese, as I told you. I'm so sorry it isn't something better."

CHAPTER 8

Lunch was extremely depressing, not only because of what it consisted of, but because of the brooding silence in which we consumed it. But no doubt it would have been worse still if anyone had tried to talk.

Gavin had a scowl on his face and seemed to be careful not to look at Hannah, as if the sight of her would have been more than he could bear. He had blamed her both for the sudden wrecking of his marriage and for the wreckage of his father's reputation, which together were certainly enough to try his temper. I did not think it impossible that the marriage could be mended, though in the mood that Gavin was in I imagined that he was convinced that this was utterly beyond hope. But if the police had left the house with the evidence in their hands that Edward Brownlow had been bribing a member of the Spellbridge council to steer contracts his way, then his reputation was certainly past saving.

Gavin too would go down in the crash. Even if he could prove that he had been against his father's paying bribes and had tried to stop it, and even if no criminal proceedings were started against him, plenty of mud would stick.

Hannah showed no sign of being disturbed by Gavin's animosity. In her way she looked serene, as if she were satisfied with what she had done. I wondered if the fact that she had told the police nothing about the existence of the letters until this morning had been on her conscience and if she felt easier in her mind now that this had been done. Doing it might have had nothing to do with a desire for revenge on Paul

Haycock. In fact, she might have kept silence for as long as she had mainly in order to shield him. But if she was unaccustomed to lying, if she was as starkly honest and upright as she appeared to be, her secret knowledge of her father's dishonesty could have been a burden that had been terrible to carry.

Yet she must have known about it for some time, or she would not have known anything at all about the letters. I wondered how long she had known about them and whether or not her present increased moodiness, the sense that she exuded of extreme unhappiness, which Gavin believed had been caused by the breakdown of her relationship with Paul Haycock, could really have been caused by the discovery of the sort of man that her beloved father was. She might even have found this out from Paul Haycock himself, if for a time the two of them had been fairly intimate. If he had assumed that she knew all about her father's concerns and had spoken of the matter casually, it might have been the very thing that had brought about the breakdown. In which case, Paul Haycock might be marrying Kay out of pique. I began to think of Kay and of how what had happened this morning could affect her and found myself feeling very sorry for her.

Felix looked deeply thoughtful. That did not necessarily mean that he was thinking deeply about anything. It could just be that it was a part of the role that he had chosen for himself at the moment. I rather hoped that it was, because when he really got thoughtful the outcome could be disquieting. If, for instance, he had seen some way that he himself could profit by the present situation and was working out how to set this in motion, it might turn out very upsetting, at least for me, because I had never been able to get over some degree of a sense of responsibility for his actions.

I do not know how I was looking myself. Worried and depressed, of course, and probably rather absent-minded. I was wishing that I could pack my suitcase, get into my car without saying good-bye to anyone, and quietly drive away. But I could not do that until I had spoken at least once more to Superintendent Hoyle. I was glad when the meal came to an end and the four of us need no longer sit around the table, trying to wear an air of detachment, but really very uneasily aware of one another, and I could help Hannah clear the table and stack the dishwasher.

We had just finished when the front doorbell rang again. It was another reporter, this time from one of the national dailies, and Felix once more dealt with him. But soon after he had left we had another visitor. Gavin went to the door and as soon as he had opened it I heard a woman's voice saying, "Gavin, Gavin, this is quite impossible! It can't go on. I won't allow it."

For a moment I thought that it was Rosie back again. Then I realized that it was Nora. Their voices were very alike, which is common in families. Gavin took her into the drawing room, where Hannah and I joined them after a moment. Felix was in his favourite place near the window. Standing there with his back to it, he contrived to appear as if he were the audience of a drama that was being performed especially for his benefit. Nora was in gum boots, trousers and an earth-stained anorak. She had a spotted red handkerchief tied over her short curly hair.

"I'm sorry about the boots," she said to Hannah as she and I came in. "I went out pretending that I was going to do some work in the garden, because Rosie insisted, absolutely *insisted*, I wasn't to come here. I think she'd have had hysterics if she'd known I meant to come. But I'd decided I had to, because someone has got to talk a little sense. So I put on my boots and my anorak and went down the garden and up across the meadow. It's pretty wet, but I wiped my feet very carefully before I came in, so I don't think I've brought any mud in with me."

Hannah looked from Nora to the door to make sure that

she had not left tracks across the polished floor, but there was nothing there of which she could complain.

"Sit down," Gavin said, doing his best to sound unconcerned, but with a great deal of eagerness under the surface. "It'll be a nice change to hear someone talk sense."

"You don't seem to have done so much of it yourself," Nora said, taking a chair by the fire, putting a strong, stubby hand on each trouser-clad knee. "To go by what Rosie said, the whole lot of you have gone mad."

"I think it was Rosie herself who went mad," Gavin said. "What's she been telling you? That I'm still in love with Kay?"

"Yes, and that she's known it in her heart all along and all that sort of thing," Nora answered. "Absolute nonsense, but the poor child's in a desperate state and won't listen to anything I say. She's been crying her eyes out."

"Crying?" Gavin said, horrified. "Not crying! I've never seen Rosie cry."

"Then you'd better come along with me and have a good look at it while it lasts," Nora said. "I haven't seen it myself for a few years, but she's making a very thorough job of it now. Anything Rosie does, she really puts her heart into."

"You want me to come along with you, do you?" Gavin asked.

"That's why I came here, isn't it?"

"But suppose she won't see me."

"I'll see she does. If she locks herself into her room, which she's been threatening to do if I dare so much as talk of her speaking to you ever again, we can provide a ladder from which you can talk to her through her window. Gavin, what on earth *did* you do that's had this shattering effect on her?"

"I only said I couldn't stand the thought of Kay marrying Paul. That's absolutely all."

"I see. That was all. Not another word of explanation."

I had not known that Nora could sound so tart.

He shifted uncomfortably from one foot to the other. "It would have been difficult to explain at the time, and she blew up so suddenly, I hadn't time to think. But she hasn't any reason to be jealous of Kay. I admit I've still got a sort of feeling—you might call it protective—about her, which may sound absurd, because she's a quite successful woman in her way. Professionally speaking, that's to say. When it comes to human relationships she's got a wonderful knack of doing the wrong thing. Marrying me was one of the wrong things she did. I wasn't nearly dynamic enough for her. I disappointed her dreadfully, though she was quite fond of me. And now she's picked on someone who she probably thinks is dynamic and all he is is a crook."

"A crook? Paul a crook?" Nora exclaimed incredulously. "I don't believe it. I've always thought him so nice."

"He's very nice," Gavin agreed. "He's friendly, good-natured and probably kind to animals. But he isn't exactly scrupulous about how he gets his money and for some time I've known a crash was coming. It was bound to. I've tried to think up ways of averting it, but I didn't have much success. And when I heard Kay was going to marry him, all I could think about was how to stop her somehow before the crash came. At the least, I thought, I ought to make sure she knew what she was in for. But Rosie didn't give me a chance to explain that, and as a matter of fact, I'm not sure I'd have told her anything about it this morning. I'd a sort of hope I could cover it up. But there's no chance of it now. The police have got the evidence and Paul will have to take what's coming to him."

Nora wrinkled her forehead. "This crash you're talking about, what do you mean?"

"Only that Paul has been taking bribes from my father to steer contracts to our firm and the police know about it and will no doubt act upon it."

"I see." Nora sat thinking about it, her eyes on Gavin's

face. After a moment she said, "Are you involved in this your-self, Gavin?"

"Up to the point that I'd found out about it but hadn't taken any action on my knowledge. I kept hoping it could be stopped. But you don't have to believe that."

"Oh, I believe you. But I'm thinking of Rosie."

"You think I ought to have told her all this before we got married?"

"Well, I rather wish you had. But of course she'll assume you're entirely innocent, you needn't worry about that, and she'll spring to your defence if you get into trouble, just so long as you can convince her you aren't yearning for Kay. If only you'd told her this straight away, it could have saved her some heartbreak. Will you come along with me now and talk to her?"

"If that's what you think I ought to do."

"Of course it is." She stood up. "Are the police going to suspect Paul now of Edward's murder? Does this give him a motive? Could it tie up in any way?"

"It's just possible," Gavin said.

"I've always liked Paul," she said. "He's so easy to get along with. But Oliver's always said he hasn't a trace of taste or intellect and hadn't any use for him. But Oliver doesn't like many people much. He's got such exacting standards. I'm afraid he'll say, 'I told you so,' when he finds out your father was, well . . ."

"Say it," Gavin said. "A crook."

A choked sound suddenly came from Hannah and, putting her hands up to her mouth, she hurried out of the room.

"Oh dear, I'm so sorry, I oughtn't to have said that," Nora said. "It must be terrible for Hannah. How much about all this has she known?"

"If you ask me, a lot more than I have," Gavin replied. "But in her eyes my father could do no wrong. Well, let's go." He put an arm round her sturdy shoulders. "I hope to

God you're right, Nora, that I'm going to be able to sort things out with Rosie. If this sorry business helps in that, I may stop worrying about it, selfish though that may be."

They went out together.

"So that's that," Felix remarked as we heard the front door close behind them. "A happy ending of sorts in view."

"Do you really think so?"

"Oh yes, I've been taking for granted all along that there'd be one sooner or later. Virginia, it's a nice day. I'm going for a walk. Do you feel like coming with me?"

I looked towards the windows and saw that the sky was still softly blue and that sunshine still lay golden on the leaf-scattered lawn. It would be pleasant, I felt, to get out of the house for a time and breathe air that was fresh and clean, untainted with crime and suspicion. But unfortunately we would take the taint with us, that was obvious. All the same, a walk seemed a good idea. However, I said that I thought I ought to make sure first that Hannah would not mind if we went out. Felix nodded and I went looking for her.

For some reason I imagined that she would have dashed upstairs to her bedroom to hide the emotions that had overcome her, but she was not there and it was in the kitchen that I finally found her. She was standing at the table, fiercely slicing an onion, and tears, the first that I had seen her shed, were streaming down her cheeks. But it was the onion that was causing the tears, not grief.

"I'm making a casserole with kidneys and red wine," she announced. "I hope you and Felix don't dislike kidneys. Some people won't touch them."

I assured her that we both liked them very much and said that Felix and I were thinking of going for a walk. She nodded briefly, then gave one of her odd laughs.

"You don't know how glad I am I'm not married," she said. "You and Felix, Gavin and Rosie, Kay and Paul, every

single one of you in a mess. I often think what a blessing it is
to be single."

I always intensely dislike being told that I had made a
mess of my marriage, since in my view it had ended up most
tidily arranged, even if the process of arranging it was painful.
But Hannah, in her single blessedness, no doubt had a far
more romantic notion of marriage than I had.

"I shouldn't think we'll be gone long," I said, "but it's such
a fine afternoon, it's tempting to go out."

"Do you like garlic?" she countered.

I said I liked it, in fact, that I liked most things, particularly if someone else had been so kind as to cook them for
me.

"And you haven't an allergy to mushrooms? There ought
to be mushrooms in this dish, but some people can't eat
them, which I think they ought to tell one before one starts
cooking. I never forgive people who don't tell one in advance
what they can't eat, when I may be meaning to take special
trouble to please them."

"It all sounds delicious."

Her cooking, I realized, was Hannah's refuge from her emotions. Some people flee to music, some to detective stories,
some go for long walks, but Hannah fled to her kitchen, sub-
merging herself in the only sensuality she allowed herself, the
thought of delectable food.

The walk on which Felix and I set out was not of the kind
that can be called a refuge from anything, but it was agreeable to be out of doors. We ambled along slowly, going down
to the bottom of the Brownlows' garden, then across the
meadow beyond it, skirting the Flints' market garden, crossing one or two more fields, then emerging onto a road that
took us through the village of Charlwood.

It was a grey stone village, most of it old, though there was
a new red box of a house near the middle of it that had the
police sign over the door, and there was a singularly unimpres-

sive church of mid-Victorian Gothic. There were two or three shops with a few cars drawn up outside them and a few people and a remarkable number of dogs in the road.

Felix and I had been almost silent as we walked along. We were at the end of the village before he remarked, "I've often wished that someone would bribe me. Not that I'd accept it unless it was a great deal of money. The pitiable thing about a lot of the cases of corruption one reads about is that people have risked their careers, their pensions, their whole futures, for a pittance. It's pathetic."

"I don't think you're in any danger of being tempted," I said. "You've nothing to offer in return."

"Oh, I don't know about that," he said. "There's always knowledge."

"Knowledge?" I did not like the sound of that. "Wouldn't that be blackmail?"

"Not if it's the other fellow who approaches one with an offer. If I approached him, I agree with you, it would be blackmail, but if it was his idea to offer me some nice sum to suppress something I knew about him, that would only be bribery."

"The distinction between the two seems rather subtle," I said. "Presumably he wouldn't make you the offer unless he thought you were going to use your knowledge against him." A very disturbing thought suddenly occurred to me. I stood still. "Felix, is there something you know about these people here that you've been keeping to yourself?"

Also standing still, he lit one of his eternal cigarettes.

"I don't know a single thing that you don't," he said.

We walked on again. In spite of the sunshine there was a nip in the air that had made itself felt as soon as we stood still. I thought that it would not be surprising if there was a frost in the evening.

"But you've got some idea in your head about it all," I said.

"I've got two or three."

"What are they?"

"No," he said, "they're nebulous in the extreme. Not worth discussing at the moment."

"Well, I hope you aren't thinking of approaching anyone with one or two of them, demanding money with menaces. We've had one murder already."

"Virginia, my love," he said gently, "I know I'm not perfect, but have you ever known me to try blackmail?"

"No, to be honest, I haven't," I replied, "but remember what our Mr. Hoyle said. There's a first time for everything." His very gentleness, instead of the annoyance which would not have been unreasonable, gave me a sickening feeling that he might have had blackmail of some curious sort on his mind.

"You're too fond of quoting Mr. Hoyle," he said, still mild. "He is not my ideal of wisdom and understanding."

"I think he's pretty acute."

"Then I wonder if he's asked himself yet just why Hannah gave him those letters of Haycock's this morning."

I had not thought about that myself. I had taken for granted that she had done it mainly for the reason that she herself had stated: that she wanted to avoid the disturbance of a police search of the house when it was certain that they would find the letters anyway. Also I thought there was a possibility that what Gavin believed was correct, that at least a part of her motive for bringing the letters to light had been a desire for revenge on Paul Haycock for whatever it was that he had done to her.

"Didn't she do it mainly to direct suspicion at Paul Haycock?" I said.

"But does it?"

"Isn't it what the police are bound to think?"

"If they do, then they aren't so very brilliant."

"I don't understand."

We had come to another standstill, then without having discussed it turned and started walking back the way we had come.

"Imagine what must have happened if you're right," Felix said. "Imagine Haycock wanting to get back the letters Brownlow was using to keep him in line. Imagine Haycock believing the Brownlow house would be empty because everyone would be at the reception in the Flints' house. So he goes to the Brownlow house and for some reason best known to himself starts hunting for the letters in Hannah's room instead of in Brownlow's study. And Brownlow, who's resting upstairs, hears a noise downstairs and comes to investigate. They come face to face. Well, why on earth should Haycock suddenly take it into his head to murder Brownlow? They'd known each other for years, Brownlow would have known exactly why Haycock had come, he'd have known Haycock hadn't got the letters because he was hunting in the wrong place, Brownlow would probably have been quite unpleasant about it and told Haycock to get out, but why should Haycock have snatched up the poker and killed him? I simply can't see it."

"They might have had a very violent quarrel. Haycock might have lost his head."

"In that case, wouldn't he have used his fists, not the poker? If it was just a case of assault, without any murderous intent, and Brownlow's death was an accident, isn't there something strange about his having picked up that poker? I think whoever did it meant to kill."

"Then you don't think it could have been Paul Haycock?"

"Oh, I haven't said that."

"I thought it's just what you have been saying."

"No, I've only said that, if he did, it wasn't on account of the letters. He might have had some other reason. But that brings me back to the question, why did Hannah hand those letters over to the police? If she'd done what Gavin said she ought to have done, made a fuss, insisted on a search warrant, delayed things, he might have had a chance of destroying them and that would have kept her father's reputation intact, anyway for a time."

"What about the fact that she's successfully made trouble for Gavin? Could that have been what she wanted to do? You know how she feels about him."

"Now that," Felix said thoughtfully, "seems to me a much more fruitful suggestion, even if it doesn't altogether answer my question, why did she hand the letters over. As long as the search went ahead without time being wasted over a search warrant, the police would have found them anyway, so why draw attention to herself by producing them so quickly?"

He had ground out the stub of his cigarette with his heel and was walking on with his hands locked behind him, his head bent and his chin sunk on his chest. I found myself wondering if there was any great detective in fiction who walked like that when he was having deep thoughts and with whom Felix was identifying himself just then, but offhand I could not think of one, though it was obvious that that was the kind of part that he was playing. We reached the point where we had first entered the village, turned off the main road and set off across the fields towards the Brownlows' house. Almost at once we saw Rosie and Gavin walking towards us.

They were hand in hand and there was a lightness about Rosie's walk, almost as if she might suddenly hop, skip and jump, which suggested that Gavin had been successful in explaining his distress at the news of Kay's engagement. Rosie had changed out of her mink and her green and white suit into jeans and an old sheepskin jacket. When we met I could see the signs of recent tears on her face, but her eyes, although they were reddened, had a sparkle in them and she greeted Felix and me with a happy smile.

"I've been such a fool, haven't I?" she said. "But perhaps it was all for the best, because now I've got all that bottled-up jealousy out of my system. I've really been appallingly jealous, you know, but not daring to say a word about it in case it turned out I was right. I mean, Kay's so beautiful and so clever and so superior to me in every way, I thought Gavin was bound to find me pretty boring soon and start wanting to get Kay back somehow. But I thought that, if I didn't say anything about it, perhaps the nasty feeling would go away, but of course it didn't, it only got worse, from the time Gavin was so depressed at lunch just after we'd got married, to the time when he lost his temper about Kay marrying Paul. But he's explained it all now and I feel such a fool for worrying the way I did, but it feels wonderful too to have that load off my mind."

Gavin looked as if he had shed several years since I had seen him last.

"I'm sorry about that lunch," he said. "I've had this bribery thing so much on my mind recently that I took for granted Stephen's call, which seemed to have something to do with Paul, must be connected with it. And if it was, if the truth was going to come out, it would mean my father was ruined. I couldn't stop thinking about it."

"Then you think Mr. Ledbetter knows about it," I said.

"I suppose he must."

"Do you think he's involved in the corruption himself?" Felix asked.

"Not to my knowledge," Gavin answered. "He's a dry, cautious man. I can't see him taking such risks."

"And Gavin never told me a thing about it!" Rosie exclaimed. "He's had all this on his mind and he's been carrying the load of it all by himself and didn't confide in me because he didn't want to make me unhappy. It'll be so much better now. We each know a lot more about the other and that's the best thing that could have happened. Well, that's not exactly what I mean, because it could have happened if we'd been sensible without any horrible murder. But at least they've caught the murderer, that's the main thing now."

"They've caught the murderer?" Felix said quickly. "Not Pete—not Bruno? They don't seriously think he did it?"

"But of course," she said. "That's simple enough, isn't it?"

"Altogether too simple," Felix replied. "He stole some silver and that's all they can prove against him. He certainly didn't search Hannah's room."

"But Mr. Hoyle has a theory about that," she said. "Gavin told me about it. He thinks this Italian had the brilliant idea of faking a search to make the murder look like an inside job."

Felix looked stern. "I know about that theory and I don't agree with it—" He stopped abruptly. For an instant there was a look of astonishment on his face. Then he carefully obliterated all expression from it. "No," he said, "I don't agree with it. It would have been too cunning to think of doing a thing like that when you'd just committed your first murder."

"How d'you know it's his first murder?" she asked.

He dismissed the question with a shrug of his shoulders. But what he had said was not what he had nearly said the moment before. He had come close to giving something quite different away, which he was anxious to keep to himself for the present.

"I think Mr. Hoyle's probably right," Rosie said. "The simplest explanation is usually the best one, isn't it? Now Gavin and I will go for our walk. It's nice to get out for a little before it gets dark. We're going home for tea, but we'll come up to the house after it."

Still hand in hand, she and Gavin went on along the path towards the village.

Felix and I went on towards the Brownlows' house. He had his hands clasped behind him again and his chin on his chest. I left him in peace to enjoy his play acting for a little while, then I said, "That theory of the superintendent's about Bruno's searching Hannah's room as a blind seems to give you ideas, even if you don't agree with it. You said so before. What are they?"

"Nothing," he said. "Nothing at all."

"Oh, come on, Felix," I said. "The others may not have noticed it, but I couldn't help seeing you'd taken yourself by surprise, suddenly thinking of something. Why not tell me what it was? You sometimes have very good ideas, but sometimes they're just horribly dangerous. I'd like to know which this one is."

"It's nothing," he said. "A mere fleeting thought. It wouldn't interest you."

"I'm sure it would."

"I haven't a shred of evidence to support it. It's just that I can see a sort of pattern emerging . . . No, you're such a one for definite evidence and solid facts and so on. There's no point in trying to explain it to you."

I could tell when he had got into one of his stubborn moods and that this was one of them. I did not waste any more breath arguing. The sun was low in the sky now and the brightness had gone from the daylight. It would soon be dusk. It was growing colder, too, with a forewarning of winter. I began to think of my own small house, which was much more comfortably warm than the Brownlows' mansion, and for the first time for the last few days I began to think of my patients and their aches and pains and their often pathetic faith in my ability to help them.

I was deeply grateful for the demands they made on me. There was something wonderfully reassuring in being needed. But I recognized that when I began to think in those terms it was a sign that I had had almost as much as I could take of Felix, who had never really needed me, even when he had convinced himself that he did, except briefly and erratically. I thought of Rosie's little homily on the therapeutic effect for a husband and wife of sharing their troubles, and of how this was something that Felix and I had never achieved. Not that we had not sometimes made a show of doing it, but one of the little difficulties about it for me had been that I had never felt sure when the troubles of which Felix told me were real or imaginary. His real ones he had usually done his best to keep to himself. I felt too that he had often found me unsatisfactory in failing to make demands on him that would have made him feel that I took him seriously.

A long time ago I had taken him utterly seriously, but after a certain point I had been careful never to do it again. Sometimes, of course, that had been a mistake, but on the whole it had been a reasonably efficient form of self-protection.

We reached the house and went to the front door and, remembering that Hannah had said that it was often left unlocked if someone was in the house, tried the handle. Today the door was locked. That, in the circumstances, was hardly surprising. Felix rang the bell. After waiting a little while, he rang it again. We could hear it pealing inside the house, but there was no sound of footsteps coming to the door.

"I hope she hasn't gone out and locked us out," Felix said. "It wouldn't be mannerly in a guest to break in, though it wouldn't be difficult."

"If we must, we can wait till Gavin gets back," I said, "but let's try the back door first."

We went round the house to the little paved yard behind it onto which the back door opened. There were two dustbins beside the door and a garden broom. The door was not locked. I pushed it open and stepped into a small scullery that contained the deep freeze and a number of storage cupboards. I went to the door that led into the kitchen.

In case the sound of our entry should alarm Hannah, I called out, "Hannah, it's us!"

Then I saw her. She was lying face downwards on the floor

between me and the table. There was a great deal of blood soaking through her brown sweater and a pool of it on the grey linoleum. Sticking out between her shoulders was what looked to me like the handle of the knife with which I had last seen her slicing onions.

CHAPTER 9

The next thing that I remember clearly was the big, bland face of Superintendent Hoyle hanging over me as I sat by the fire in the drawing room. That does not mean that I had been unconscious all that time. I do not think that I had been unconscious at all. But there had been a great deal of confusion in my mind, a sense of people coming and going without my being sure who they were, of voices arguing and of my own saying quite lucidly that Hannah had been going to make a casserole of kidneys in red wine, but that she did not seem to have got much further with it after I had left her because, although she had apparently finished slicing the onions for it, she had not even begun on the kidneys and mushrooms.

It was Felix who had pushed me into the drawing room and made me sit down by the fire, which was almost out, to keep me from getting in the way of the policemen. He had put two or three logs on the fire and stirred it up and by the time that Mr. Hoyle came in to talk to me there was a good blaze crackling on the hearth. Felix had kept his head surprisingly well. He had not had to dash out anywhere to be sick, but had calmly telephoned the police and then Nora, asking her to tell Gavin what had happened. Then he had talked to someone else on the telephone, I was not sure who, though I had had a feeling that it was Kay, but I had not paid any attention to what he had said.

Gavin and Rosie arrived a few minutes before the police and it had been Gavin who greeted the superintendent and took him into the kitchen, though after that Felix and I had

had to describe how we had found Hannah's body and account for our actions from the time that Gavin and Nora had left the house. There was no one to corroborate our statements that Hannah had still been alive when we left it, nor any witness to my conversation with her about the casserole that she had been preparing, so we were possible suspects, but I do not think the thought of this worried me. I only felt extremely anxious, for some reason, that the police should understand the significance of the kidneys and mushrooms that Hannah had not begun to slice. There was also the matter of the half bottle of Médoc on the kitchen table, the cork of which had not been drawn.

"I see what you mean," Mr. Hoyle said as he loomed over me in the drawing room. "She'd got hardly any further with her preparations after you went out before something interrupted her. Something or someone—the murderer, presumably. You think he got here only a few minutes after you left, though you can't tell how long they talked before he drove that knife into her. You can't tell either whether or not she knew she was talking to a murderer."

"But there's one thing you can be sure of," Felix said, coming into the room just then, "and that is that it wasn't Bruno."

"Yes," Mr. Hoyle agreed, "we shan't be charging him with murder. But there's a possibility we ought to consider, in my view. Mrs. Freer, you say that after Mrs. Flint and Mr. Brownlow left the house you and your husband decided to go for a walk, that you had a few minutes' talk with Miss Brownlow, then you went out. Well, wasn't that the first time Miss Brownlow had been alone in the house all day?"

"Yes," I said. "So the murderer must have seen us leave and come in as soon as we'd gone."

"Possibly, oh yes, possibly. But it might not have happened like that at all. What might have happened, it seems to me, is that Miss Brownlow seized that moment to make a telephone call. It was the first time she'd had a chance to do it. There are two extensions upstairs, besides the telephone in the hall, one in her own bedroom and one in her father's study, and you'd think that if she'd wanted to make a call she might have used one of them, but if it was something very confidential indeed that she wanted to talk about, she might have been scared of someone listening in as long as there was anyone at all in the house. But once you'd gone, she might have abandoned her cooking at once and gone to the telephone."

"What you're saying is that she knew who the murderer was," I said, "and wanted to talk to him."

"I'm only saying it's a possibility. And a part of its importance, if that's what happened, is that it may affect the alibis of a number of people, because the murderer would have taken a little time to get here after she summoned him, so the murder may have happened rather later than it would appear if we accept your interpretation of the evidence."

"But do you really think she knew who killed her father and kept silent about it?" I asked.

"Well, it's a queer thing, but that's exactly what I do think," he answered. "I don't know just why, but all along I've felt that woman knew something. There was something about the way she gave us those letters this morning that puzzled me. And even yesterday evening I had that feeling about her, though I couldn't have told you why."

"But surely she wouldn't have made an appointment with someone she knew was a murderer."

"You'd think not, unless she had a reason to think herself safe."

Felix said, "In other words, that she was his accomplice."

But the superintendent seemed to dislike having the matter put to him so baldly and, muttering that that was going much too fast, hurried out of the room.

I wondered how seriously Felix took the idea that Hannah could have been the murderer's accomplice. I could not believe in it myself. I was more ready to agree with the superintendent that she had known something about her father's murder which she had been keeping to herself, because that supplied such a simple motive for her own murder. But would she have kept it to herself unless she was somehow involved in it? Was there anyone she cared about enough to protect him?

"Where are Gavin and Rosie?" I asked Felix.

"Upstairs," he answered. "I think they're packing their suitcases. Two murders seem to be a bit too much for Rosie to take. I think they're going to move out and spend the night at the Flints'."

"Then you and I could move to a hotel in Spellbridge," I said. "The police will probably be quite glad if the house is left empty."

Felix looked uncertain. "Is that what you want to do?"

"Wouldn't it be best?"

"Perhaps it would. On the other hand . . ."

"Yes?" I said as he paused.

"Let's think about it."

I had thought that he would jump at the suggestion and as my habit was, whenever he acted in a way that I was not expecting, I started to wonder what there was behind it. Was there anything in it for Felix?

"I think I'd sooner go to a hotel than stay here," I said. "I remember your saying when we first got here that this house had a bad atmosphere. I hadn't noticed it specially at the time, but now it seems to me a grave understatement."

"Then go to a hotel, if you want to," he said.

"Don't you want to come too?"

"You know I hate hotels."

This was untrue. From the smallest, homeliest pub to the most sophisticated of great modern hotels, I knew that he enjoyed staying in them, because he loved being waited on. When it happened he always acted as if he were accustomed to it every day of his life and was always gracious and generous. It was true that the hotels in Spellbridge were probably of the stolid railway type and might not appeal to him, but it was hardly likely that this was his reason for wanting to stay in a house where he would have to look after himself and where two murders had been committed.

"If you're staying here, I'd better stay too," I said.

"There's really no need, if you'd sooner leave."

"I'd much sooner leave, but I'm not going without you."

"Why not? I'll be quite all right alone."

"Of course you will, but will the house? You're up to something. I don't know what it is but, until I do, I'm staying."

"Just as you like." He stooped, picked up the poker and prodded the fire into even brighter flames. Then, absently, he changed his grip on the poker, grasping it firmly and seeming for a moment, as he looked down at it, to be wondering how it would feel to lift it high and bring it down with enough force to smash something, such, for instance, as an undefended skull. The effect of that, however, was to make him shudder sharply and put the poker down hurriedly on the hearth.

"Felix, you really shouldn't try to be a detective," I said. "You haven't the right sort of toughness. I should leave the job to the police."

"One doesn't have to be tough to use one's brains," he answered. "But I think I agree with you now, your Mr. Hoyle is quite acute. More so than I thought at first. That guess of his that Hannah made a telephone call after we left the house was pretty shrewd."

"You think she actually rang up the murderer and asked him to come here?" I said. "You think she knew who killed her father?"

"Oh, I'm fairly certain she knew that, but I don't think it was the murderer she telephoned, I think it was Kay."

"Why do you think that?"

"Because I telephoned Kay myself just before the police got here to tell her that Hannah had handed Haycock's letters over to them. I thought it was only decent to warn her that he'd got trouble coming. And I found she already knew about their having the letters, and how could she have known that unless Hannah had phoned her?"

"Gavin might have done it."

"I asked him if he had when he and Rosie first got here and he said he hadn't and there's no reason why he should lie about it."

"But why should Hannah do it?"

"You know she always had a soft spot for Kay. She couldn't help admiring her. And it may have been on her conscience that she'd wrecked Kay's chances of a happy marriage."

"That was on her conscience, but her father's murder wasn't?"

Felix smiled. "Oh, I think it was. I don't think for a moment she was the murderer's accomplice. When I suggested that, it was just taking the superintendent's theory to its logical conclusion, but of course it's wrong."

"You said he was acute."

"So he is, but you can be acute and still be wrong. Anyway, he was supposing that she'd rung up the murderer and invited him to come here, which she didn't."

"How can you be sure? She might have made two telephone calls."

"Think over that scene in the kitchen. You've kept harping on that yourself, even if you aren't sure why. Remember, you went in there and you saw her slicing up onions. Then you and I went out and were gone for quite a while, yet when we came back and found her dead, her preparations hadn't got any farther than when we left. And you know the kind of person she was. She was a compulsive cook. Even if she'd telephoned the murderer and been waiting for him, she wouldn't have sat doing nothing. She'd have gone back to the kitchen and got on with her job. She'd have sliced up the kidneys and mushrooms and drawn the cork of her bottle of wine. None of which she did."

"So you think he interrupted her before she could get started again."

"I think he was waiting for her in the kitchen when she got back from making her telephone call to Kay. I think he'd seen Gavin and Nora leave, then you and me, and he knew she was in the house alone. And he came in by the back door and there in front of him on the kitchen table was the perfect weapon for the murder he'd planned. That kitchen knife. And he picked it up and waited for her and when she came in he plunged the knife into her immediately and left in a hurry, because we might have come back at any time. Of course, when he came in he couldn't have known the knife would be there, or that she'd be at work in the kitchen, so the chances are he brought some weapon with him, or planned to use the poker again. After all, she might have been sitting in here, or have been lying down upstairs, or anywhere. He might have had to hunt for her through the house. But as things turned out, they couldn't have been more convenient for him."

"But why should he have killed her, if she was shielding him?"

"I don't think she was shielding him."

"But if she knew who he was and said nothing . . ."

"From what I know of Hannah," Felix said, "I think she meant to inflict her own kind of punishment. Think of those bank statements of hers, Virginia. Don't they tell you anything?"

I gave a slow shake of my head. My mind was not functioning at its best, but even if it had been, I doubt if I should have been able to follow him. All I could think of just then was that he was sure who the murderer was and that if he had a grain of sense he would tell this at once to the police and that his only reason for not doing so was his violent and un-reasonable prejudice against them. Also, perhaps, there was his vanity. If he could present them with a complete solution of the case before they had found one themselves, it would be a way of scoring off them.

I tried to argue with him. "If you know something, Felix, why don't you tell Mr. Hoyle?"

"Because I haven't the necessary evidence yet," he answered.

"But you expect to find it. You expect to find it tonight. You're going to make another search of the house as soon as the police leave, that's why you won't move out to a hotel."

"I told you there's no need for you to stay," he said.

"Oh, this time when you search I'll be right behind you. But why can't you tell me now whom you suspect?"

"I will when I've got the evidence."

"No, tell me now."

I could see that for a moment he wavered. I thought that really he was bursting to tell me his theory, because he was so delighted with it. But at the same time there was a great deal of pleasure for him in tantalizing me, putting on the act that evidence, of all dull things, mattered so greatly to him, when the truth was that imagination always mattered so much more. Torn between the two impulses, he hesitated, and in the silence the front doorbell rang.

It was some time before we knew who had come to the house, but presently Kay came into the room. A policeman had let her in and taken her to be interviewed by the superintendent. For the first time since I had known her, I thought that she had suddenly lost her beauty. The bones of her thin face seemed too near the surface and the skin was strained so tightly over them that it showed the beginning of wrinkles. She was wearing the same raincoat as the evening before, but her head was bare, with her dark chestnut hair pushed carelessly back behind her ears.

"Why in hell did I ever come to this bloody town?" she demanded. "Why didn't I know there'd be no luck in it for me?"

She looked questioningly at Felix and me, as if she expected an answer.

When neither of us said anything, she threw herself down on the sofa.

"Why do I always make a mess of everything?" she went on. "Why can't I just for once do the right thing?"

"What have you done now?" Felix asked, sitting down beside her. "Coming to this house this evening? Is there something wrong about that?"

She brushed that aside impatiently. "Thinking that I could pick a man whom I could love and stick to," she said. "Can you imagine that? Me! But that's what I wanted and it's what I thought I'd done. I thought I'd found someone solid and reliable with whom I could settle down and be happy and share a home and perhaps even adopt a couple of children, because it's a little late in the day to think of producing any myself, and get out of the rat race. That's honestly what I wanted and what I believed I'd got. And what does this solid and reliable character turn out to be? A cheap crook."

Her face was drawn and her voice was desperate.

"I suppose you're right, that's what he is," Felix said, picking up one of her hands and holding it comfortingly. "I suppose taking bribes is a crime. But there are much worse things."

"Oh yes, like murder." She was mocking, but she left her hand in his. "One mustn't lose one's sense of proportion. There are big crimes and little crimes. And as I happen to know, he isn't a murderer. I can give him an alibi for yesterday afternoon and for this horrible thing today as well. He's just a small, mean crook who's had his hand in the till. What I took for honest respectability, which is something that at long last I've come to admire, is just hypocrisy."

Thinner Than Water

She was thinking about herself a great deal more than about Hannah, which was not surprising, because she had always been deeply egotistic, but I was interested in what she had said about Paul Haycock's alibi.

"Were you together all this afternoon?" I asked.

"Most of it, after he got back from the office," she said. "He left about an hour ago and the police told me Hannah was killed long before that. He took the car, of course, so I had to get a taxi to come out here."

"What d'you mean, he left?" Felix asked. "Where's he gone?"

"I haven't the least idea," she answered. "He just said it would be best for him to clear out fast and he slung some clothes into a suitcase, pocketed a fair amount of money that I think he'd been keeping in the flat in case of an emergency like this, and bolted."

"You mean he's run out on you," Felix said.

"Of course I mean he's run out on me!" she snarled. "Isn't that what I'm telling you?"

"And it's that that you can't forgive." Felix nodded with an air of sudden understanding, as if he had not taken her horror at Paul Haycock's having accepted bribes altogether seriously. "How did it all happen?"

"It began with Hannah telephoning me," she said. "I was in Paul's flat, waiting for him, and she rang up, I'm not sure just when, but it was sometime in the early afternoon, and she told me she wanted to warn me she'd handed Paul's letters to her father to the police. I asked, what letters, and she told me then about the bribes, and she said she wanted me to know what she'd done so that I could get away if I wanted before the storm broke over Paul's head. Of course I didn't want to. I'd every intention of standing by him and I told him so as soon as he got home. I really meant it. I said if he was arrested and went to prison I'd wait for him and all sorts of absurd things. I don't know if I really would have when it came to the point, but that's how I felt at the time, while I was still stunned and hadn't thought anything out. And he just started packing a suitcase and said he was getting out. He said he's a bank account somewhere abroad and he'd be all right and I wasn't to worry about him. Worry! Me worry about him! A lot he was worrying about me! He didn't even ask me to go with him."

"Would you have gone if he had?" Felix asked.

She drew a deep breath, then deliberately made herself relax. After a moment she said, "Probably not. Or if I had, I'd have regretted it and got out later. I expect he knew that. I hadn't been counting on a life of bolting and hiding, changing our names perhaps and all that kind of thing, as I imagine we'd have had to do. Or if it wouldn't have been quite as bad as that, at least we shouldn't have been able to come home again. It's beginning to look funny to me now, but what I really believed I wanted was a quiet life of coffee mornings and sedate little cocktail parties and occasional formal luncheons where I'd be someone because I was the wife of the chairman of the Housing and Development Committee, and I even thought of taking up golf. It just shows one shouldn't ever try to get away from oneself, because that's all I was doing. I was bound to make a bad choice, because I was right out of my depth."

"I know just how you feel," Felix said. "It was more or less the same when I married Virginia. I thought with her common sense and levelheadedness she could cure me of being the sort of person I was. A very bad reason for marriage and very unfair to her, since I didn't really want to be cured."

I thought that was going rather far.

"I'd sooner you didn't confuse me with Paul Haycock," I said. "I've never taken a bribe."

"I'm not saying you have," Felix said. "I'm only saying Kay and I have a certain amount in common."

Jealousy is a peculiar emotion. I had no right on earth to feel jealous if Felix was attracted to Kay and trying to make an impression on her. I had refused to live with him for several years and I knew that during that time he had had a number of love affairs for which, on the whole, I had been grateful, as they had relieved me of a sense that I might have had that I had irremediably ruined his life. I liked him to be happy and occupied. But I had never had to sit looking on while he showed his awakening interest in another woman, or see her gradual response to him.

I thought, from the look of her, that Kay was beginning to remember that once upon a time, long ago, she and Felix had been close to falling in love and she was wondering whether now, in their maturity, they might not have more to share with one another than they had had then. If so, I admitted to myself, that was strictly their business and nothing to do with me. Yet I had to stifle some feeling that was threatening my composure.

"You say that Paul Haycock spent the afternoon in his office, Kay," I said. "How sure can you be of that?"

"The police confirmed it as soon as I told them about it," she said. "They telephoned one of the other partners in the firm and apparently he said that Paul was at a meeting all the afternoon. He was in the office all day, except for lunch, which he had with me in the same pub we went to yesterday."

"What brought you out here today?" I asked. "Felix must have told you what had happened to Hannah."

She nodded. "I just felt I had to talk to somebody when Paul went off like that. I couldn't stand staying alone in the flat and the police had asked me not to leave Spellbridge yet."

"A thing I've been wondering about," Felix said, "were Haycock and Hannah ever in love?"

She looked puzzled. "What makes you ask that?"

"Only that Gavin seems to think they were."

"Then I'd ask him about it, if you think it's important."

"You didn't ever think so yourself?"

"I can't answer for Hannah's feelings, but I don't think there was anything on Paul's side. But as a matter of fact . . ." She paused suddenly as though some thought had struck her.

"Yes?" Felix said.

"When I met her last, which was more than a year ago in London," Kay said, "she told me she might be going to get married. Then she seemed to wish she hadn't said it and wouldn't answer a single question about it, so I began to think it might be just some kind of daydream she was nursing, and when I didn't hear any more about it I forgot all about it until this moment. It never occurred to me it might be Paul she was thinking of. He was my lover by then and we were already toying with the thought of getting married."

"You don't think he might have been stringing her along, hoping to persuade her to rescue his letters from her father for him?" Felix suggested.

"I suppose it isn't impossible," she said. "Now that I've found out what a louse he is, I feel he might be capable of anything."

"If anyone was stringing anyone along," I said, "I think Hannah was doing it to Paul. She may have let him think that she could be persuaded to get him the letters, and he may have believed that he mattered to her, but really she seemed delighted to hear you and he were getting married, at least partly because she thought it would be a great embarrassment to Gavin to have you living so near him."

"But she did tell me she might be getting married," Kay said. "If it wasn't Paul, who was it?"

As she said it, the front doorbell rang again.

One of the policemen went to answer it and, while he was talking to the new arrival at the door, Rosie and Gavin came into the room. They were wearing coats and carrying suit-cases.

"Hello, Kay," Gavin said without surprise at seeing her. He was probably past being surprised by anything. "What are you doing here?"

"Just dropped in for a comfortable chat," she answered ironically. "Where are you going?"

He appeared to find her explanation of her presence ade-quate. He looked confused and bewildered, but resigned to accepting the inexplicable.

"I've persuaded Rosie to go home," he said. "I'll take her over there, then come back, in case I'm wanted."

"D'you mean you'll be staying the night here?" The anxi-ety in Felix's voice would not have been apparent to anyone there but me, but it told me how eager he was to have the house to himself.

"No, I'll go back to the Flints' later," Gavin answered. "Are you and Virginia staying here or going to a hotel?"

"Staying here, if you don't mind," Felix said.

"Stay as long as you like. I don't think it's what I'd do in your place. I'd want to get out as soon as I could. But you're welcome to stay if you want to."

I asked, "Who was that at the door just now, Gavin?"

"At the door?" He frowned, as if it took an effort of mem-ory to think clearly as far back as the ringing of the doorbell, though he must have seen who had arrived. "Oh, that was Stephen. I think the police sent for him. He seemed to know what had happened to Hannah. He's with Hoyle now. Well, I'll be seeing you presently."

He and Rosie went out. All the time that they had been in the room Rosie had been eyeing Kay with a gaze of quiet assessment, and what she had seen had seemed to puzzle her. I did not know if they had ever met before. Gavin had not in-troduced them, which suggested that they had, yet in the mood that he was in it might simply not have occurred to him to do so. If they had not met till now, and if Rosie was looking for the legendary beauty of whom she had heard and whom she feared, she would have seen very little of her in the haggard, middle-aged woman on the sofa. A look that might have been pity had appeared in her golden-brown eyes. Her youth, instead of making her vulnerable, had suddenly made her feel sure of herself.

"Stephen," Kay said. "Stephen Ledbetter, the family solicitor. I remember him. I saw him once when Gavin and I were making our wills. We did that when we got married. We each left everything we had to the other. In my case that meant just a few oddments of furniture and jewellery, but Gavin had the money he'd inherited from his mother. We'd got through that by the time we separated, which I believe was why he went into his father's firm. But he'll be quite rich now, won't he? He'll inherit whatever his father left, which I should think is a good deal, and there's this house, which will fetch an enormous amount at present prices, and he may inherit what Hannah had too. She wasn't the kind of person who'd get through her capital as we got through his. Living at home, she'd have had no need to. I think I ought to have stuck to Gavin. At my time of life it would be comforting to be married to a rich man."

"I suppose Gavin will be pretty well off," Felix said, "if the corruption scandal doesn't bust the firm. But I think it will. Even so, he won't be exactly poverty-stricken, and if he goes to gaol he won't get a long sentence. Personally, I think he'll get off altogether."

"If he does go to gaol," Kay said, "will Rosie stick to him, do you think?"

"Oh yes, for sure," he said. "She's the type."

"So he stands to gain quite a lot by these murders," she said, "because, if Hannah made a will, she probably left what she had to her father. There was no one else she cared about. So it'll come to Gavin in the end. And when the police are looking for a murderer, isn't their first question always—who benefits?"

"Gavin the murderer!" I exclaimed. "Are you raving?"

The door opened and Stephen Ledbetter came in. He had overheard us.

"I wish the police were as sure as you are, Mrs. Freer, that Mrs. Brownlow's raving," he said. "It's my impression that Gavin is their favourite suspect."

Seeing him standing in the doorway with his stern, ascetic face looking strained and worn, something about him struck me that had not done so before, and that was that he was a handsome man with great dignity, who in a cadaverous way was very impressive. A thought that I had had about him a moment before came back to me and seemed more credible than it had when it first came into my head. It was simply that, if some time ago Hannah had thought that she was going to get married, Stephen Ledbetter might have been the man in the case. He would have made an admirable father figure and it would have been like her, I thought, to have set her heart on someone like him rather than on someone nearer her own age. Besides that, he was a widower whose children had grown up and gone away, so that they would not be under her feet, needing the affection of which she had so little to give, and no doubt he was lonely, which might have given her a fellow feeling for him.

Not that anything had come of it, even if my guess at how she had felt about him was right. She could have changed her mind and decided that marriage was not what she wanted after all, or he might not have responded to her, or even been aware that in her imagination he had become her lover. And this guess of mine, right or wrong, did not help in the least in solving the murder. What had happened, or not happened, between Hannah and Stephen Ledbetter a year ago could have no connection that I could see with what had happened to her and her father during the last two days.

The lawyer walked forward to the fire and held out his hands to it. They were fine, slender hands with the freckles of age on their backs and were trembling slightly.

"This must have been a shock for you all, a terrible shock," he said. "Poor Hannah—poor, dear Hannah. I've known her since she was a child. A beautiful child, though she was always painfully shy. My wife was very attached to her. She used to ask her and Gavin to our house to play with our children, but she'd never join in, or if she did she'd get wildly overexcited and it nearly always ended in tears. Poor girl, such a fearful end. I suppose she knew something that she was keeping to herself. I wonder why she'd do that."

"Do you think the police seriously believe Gavin's responsible for those two murders?" Felix asked.

"Oh, they've no real evidence against him," Ledbetter answered. "But it seemed to me just now that that was how their minds were working. They think they've found a motive. Ever since they found out this morning that Edward had been bribing Paul and that Gavin knew about it, they've believed he knew the firm was going to go smash and that he'd be out of a job, just when he needed one. But with his father dead he stood to inherit a fair amount of money. And he knew his father was at home yesterday afternoon, waiting for me. If he and his wife had come straight here when they left the reception, he could have done it. She, of course, would have had to be in on it, but the police seem to assume that you can expect the young to be callous and violent. Then this afternoon, if he'd seen you and your wife, Mr. Freer, go out for your walk after he'd reached the Flints' house, he'd have known Hannah was alone and he could have come straight back and killed her. It's against him, unfortunately, that Hannah kept what she knew to herself. They think she might have done that for a brother."

"Not in this family!" I said. "Not Hannah!"

"But this is frightful!" Felix exclaimed, his thoughts

immediately dominated by his usual passionate loyalty to his friends. "This has got to be sorted out. We can't let them go on thinking that kind of thing about Gavin and Rosie. Mr. Ledbetter, yesterday you told us you came here in the afternoon because Mr. Brownlow wanted very urgently to change his will. I assume there wasn't much truth in that."

"Not a word." The solicitor gave a crooked smile. "It was I who urgently wanted to see him, but I hoped not to have to explain that to the police, as the facts about his bribing of Haycock hadn't come out yet. My story about his wanting to change his will was all that I could think of on the spur of the moment. The truth was that I wanted to warn him that his bribery had been discovered. I didn't think that a warning could help him much. He was too deep in to be able to pull out. But at least it would prepare him for the shock. He was a very old friend, as well as a client. I wanted to do what I could."

There was great sadness in his voice, as well as more warmth than I would have expected of him.

"How did you come to hear of it yourself?" Felix asked.

"One of my partners is on the council," Ledbetter replied. "The facts had been laid before them by a new young clerk who'd been going through the correspondence of the last few years to bring himself up to date about his own work, and what he'd uncovered could have only one interpretation. I heard about it from my partner yesterday morning, and I rang up and insisted on seeing Edward later in the day. I thought it best to talk privately out here, instead of risking being overheard in his office or mine, but I'd a full day ahead of me and I couldn't get here till later in the afternoon than I'd expected. I wish to God now I'd let some of my work wait. None of it seems important any longer. But, as I understood it, the council weren't going to act immediately. They wanted more evidence first. So although the matter was urgent it didn't seem desperate." He gave a deep sigh. "I'll be getting home now. I've told the police all I can. I can't do anything more."

"If you're going back into Spellbridge now, Mr. Ledbetter," Kay said, standing up, "could you give me a lift? I haven't a car. I came out by taxi."

"Of course," he said.

He opened the door for her and they went out together.

Soon afterwards Gavin reappeared, distraught, abstracted and with no desire to talk to anybody. He had several drinks and sat glowering at the fire with his lips moving occasionally in what looked like silent curses. All of a sudden he stood up, pushed his fingers through his grey hair and strode out of the room. I thought that there was something almost to be expected in his having got himself suspected of murder. For as long as I had known him he had had a knack of getting himself into trouble, yet it never seemed to be his own fault. It was just something that happened to him. There seem to be people like that. He did not come back, so I assumed that he had been permitted to rejoin Rosie at the Flints' house.

I did not notice what time it was that the police finally left. Hannah's body had been taken away some time before. The police surgeon had come and gone and so had the fingerprint men and the photographer. Mr. Hoyle came to say good night to Felix and me, asked if we were staying in the house, said that he expected to see us in the morning, then he went too. Without any obvious reason for being there at all, Felix and I had the place to ourselves.

As soon as he was sure of that, Felix moved swiftly. He went straight upstairs with me at his heels. I thought that he would make for Edward Brownlow's study, but it was to Hannah's bedroom that he went. It was an unexpectedly feminine room, of the kind that has a great deal too much pink in the curtains and carpet, a dressing table with a deep flowered frill round it and an unnecessary number of mirrors, so that, wherever I looked, I saw my own face reflected back at me. The only picture in the room was a large photograph of Edward Brownlow in a silver frame.

Felix stood still in the middle of the room, looking round. "Now where," he said, "would a woman put . . . ?"

As he stopped, chewing his upper lip, I said, "If you'd tell me what you're looking for, perhaps I could help."

He frowned, as if I had interrupted some train of thought, and did not answer.

Then he went suddenly to a chest of drawers and started pulling the drawers out, one after the other, not looking at what was in them, but at the back of them, as if he expected to find something taped there. It was only when he found that there was nothing that he went hurriedly through the contents of the drawers, but without giving them much attention, and evidently he did not find what he was looking for, because he pushed them back into their places.

After that he went to a tall wardrobe, pulled it open, started dragging down odd cardboard boxes from a high shelf and riffling hastily and not very hopefully through them. He did not trouble to put them back where they had come from but left them lying on the floor. Then he climbed onto a chair and took a look at the top of the wardrobe.

In the middle of doing that he gave a sudden exclamation, but it was not because of anything that he had found up there. It was because of something that had just come into his head. Jumping down from the chair, he went straight across the room to the picture of Edward Brownlow, picked it up and turned it over and in a moment had the back of the frame off it. What he took out was another photograph.

"My God, what a place to hide it!" he exclaimed. "There's a certain irony in it."

He held it out to me.

It was a photograph of a man and a woman, both half naked, so that it looked as if they had been so impatient in their desire for one another that they had not waited to undress fully. They were lying on some kind of couch. There was no difficulty in recognizing them. They were Hannah and Oliver Flint.

CHAPTER 10

"But I don't understand how you knew what to look for," I said.

Felix and I were in the bar of the White Horse, a small pub in the village of Charlwood which luckily for us provided food of a kind. It was almost closing time, but we had been supplied with cottage pie and peas and glasses of what claimed to be claret. We had ventured out in the dark along the unlit street of the village in the hope of finding somewhere where we could eat, because neither of us had the stomach even to warm up a tin of beans in the kitchen where Hannah had been murdered, where chalk marks on the floor still showed the outlines of her body and where a coating of the dust distributed by the fingerprint men lay over everything. Yet we had not felt like going to bed hungry.

A nearly full moon had made the walk to the pub not too difficult, though the ground underfoot had been treacherous, for the frost that I had foreseen had made the puddles left behind by yesterday's rain very slippery and I had clutched at Felix's arm more than once as we walked along to save myself from falling. We had seen that a notice in the window of the White Horse advertised snacks, had turned into it and accepted what we were offered.

"There were three things that did it," Felix said. "Hoyle's idea that my old friend Pete faked that search of Hannah's room, her bank statements and the way she handed over her father's letters."

I shook my head. "That doesn't convey anything to me."

"I somehow liked that idea of Hoyle's," he said. "It seemed to mean something to me, though I knew it was wrong. Pete isn't up to thinking of a subtle thing like that. But what it would have meant, if Hoyle had been right, was that Pete had, so to speak, put the obvious pattern of things into reverse. Instead of the silver having been taken to distract attention from the search in Hannah's room, it would have meant that the search had been made just to make us think that. And that started me thinking of other things in reverse. Blackmail, for instance."

"How can blackmail go into reverse?"

"When the victim begins to blackmail the blackmailer."

I scooped some tinned peas onto my fork. "How could that be possible?"

"If there was a piece of evidence in existence which the victim could use against the blackmailer, given the right circumstances."

"Go on."

"It was those bank statements of Hannah's that made me think of it. For a considerable period she'd been paying out five hundred a month that she couldn't afford for some reason that she'd apparently kept very secret. So naturally I thought of blackmail. But then those payments stopped and someone began to pay her five hundred a month instead. And that happened last Easter, at just about the time the Flints came into money. D'you remember, we wondered if Hannah could have been helping the Flints on the quiet and they'd started paying her back, only we didn't feel she was the sort of person who'd have done that. And if she wasn't, I thought, mightn't those payments to her be blackmail? But if they were, it meant the evidence the blackmailer had been using against her could be turned against him, and that's when I first thought of a photograph with two people in it."

"I don't follow," I said.

He was patient with my slowness. "Well, suppose someone

had a very compromising photograph of Hannah which he threatened to show her father if she didn't pay him five hundred for it. You know the sort of man her father was and the sort of feeling she had about him. She may have loved him, but she didn't trust him. There wasn't any trust to spare in the Brownlow family. The old man wouldn't have been understanding or helpful, as I suppose some fathers might have been. Not mine, but I'm told there are fathers like that. And his horror when he found out what had been going on would have been agony for her. So, being basically a rather simple soul, she made the mistake of most people who submit to blackmail and paid the five hundred and thought she'd be given the photograph. But all she was given was a print. Flint naturally kept the negative. It may have been a kind of spitefulness that made him give her the print, to remind her of the hold he had on her. Then he began his demands for five hundred every month and the foolish woman paid up. And I suppose she'd have gone on doing that till her money was gone and God knows what she'd have done then—killed herself, perhaps. But, as it happened, the Flints came into money and the whole situation changed."

"Because Oliver Flint didn't need the money anymore?"

"No, because Hannah only had to show that print she'd got to Nora for the Flint marriage to be washed up. And Flint would have found himself lacking a rich wife. A wife who gives the impression of being very much in love with him and who'd be hurt to the core if she found he was unfaithful. He knows her better than we do and he may have known she'd be unforgiving. And so no nice home in Portugal for Oliver, and no more sitting back, having fun with his hobbies, while she did all the hard work. So Flint began to pay Hannah. My guess about her is that, when he'd returned the money she'd paid him, she'd have called it off. She hadn't a criminal mind. She was only doing what she thought was justified. But we'll never know if I'm right about that, because the murder happened."

I had finished my cottage pie and peas and was sipping at the red fluid in my glass.

"Oliver was supposed to be in his studio, wasn't he, when Hannah arrived at the Flints' house to help Nora before the reception?" I said. "So he didn't hear her tell Nora that her father wasn't coming to it. He's one of the people who'd have believed the Brownlows' house was empty. So I imagine he went up to it across the fields and didn't meet anyone, and of course got into the house easily, as the door wasn't locked, though that ought to have warned him that there was someone in the house, and he went straight to Hannah's room and started searching for the print. And Edward Brownlow heard him and came to see what was going on. But why did Oliver have to murder him? Couldn't he have made up some story about what he was doing there?"

"Can you think of one? Hannah would have heard from her father how he'd caught Flint going through her papers and that might have driven her to do the very thing he was afraid of: show the print to Nora. And to spur Flint on, he and Brownlow had always detested one another. There may have been some really violent quarrel before Flint grabbed the poker."

"And you worked all this out from Hannah's bank statement," I said. "Felix, why did you never put your intelligence to some useful purpose? You could have done almost anything if you'd ever really tried."

But I ought to have known that that was a subject that he would never discuss. He was more satisfied than most people are with his life as it was.

He went on, "You're forgetting the way Hannah handed over her father's letters from Haycock to Hoyle. I could think of only one reason why she should do that, and that was simply that she didn't want the police to make any search of the house. Giving them the letters put a stop to that. So somewhere in the house, I thought, she'd got something hidden that was at the bottom of everything that had happened, and I already had the thought of a photograph in my mind, and her bedroom seemed to me the likeliest place for her to keep it. But I couldn't search for it there while she was around."

"Was it because you were thinking of a photograph that you let Oliver take yours?" I asked.

"Of course."

"But you didn't learn anything from it, did you?"

"Not much, except that he's a very fine photographer. There was genius in his really frightening portrait of Hannah. But there was also that charming family group of himself and Nora and Rosie that I told you about. I didn't think of it at the time, but later I guessed that he'd taken it himself by remote control, so to speak, and he must have managed the photograph of himself and Hannah in the same way, without her having any suspicion that he was doing it. That couch they were on, by the way, is in the studio."

"How did she ever get involved with him?" I said. "How could it ever have happened?"

Felix shrugged his shoulders. "You know what people are. You ought never to be surprised at anything they do."

"No." I had a feeling that, instead of being in the least surprised, I ought to have understood the situation from the beginning. There had been clues enough. I ought to have recognized that Hannah was a passionate woman. There had been passion in her love for her father and in her jealous hatred of Gavin. She had even put passion into her cooking and the way that she had kept the house. But she had been friendless and desperately lonely and terribly shy and had tried to cover it up with a sort of aggressiveness. And she had had money. Not a great deal, but some. She had been the perfect victim for a man like Oliver Flint. He had made love to her and had got her to believe that he would leave his wife and marry her.

I remembered that she had told Kay that she was thinking of getting married, and also I remembered Gavin's belief that she had been in love and had been rejected, though he had been wrong about who the man was. And all the time Oliver Flint had simply been waiting for an opportunity to set her up for that photograph.

No wonder that she had had her obsession that money was the only thing that anybody ever wanted, that Gavin could not possibly be genuinely in love with Rosie but only wanted her money. Poor Hannah had thought for a time that her love was what Oliver Flint wanted, then had found out, in the cruelest way imaginable, that it had only been her five hundred a month.

"But why did Oliver have to murder her?" I asked. "He'd got power over her, she'd got power over him. They could have called it quits."

"He could never have trusted her," Felix said. "I don't think for a moment she meant to let him get away with her father's murder. Even if it had meant letting the police see that photograph, I think she'd have turned him in in the end. Or that's what he must have believed. Once he'd made the mistake of committing the first murder, he was in her hands. After all, it was the thought of her father seeing the photograph that really horrified her and once he was dead it may not have mattered to her much what anybody else thought. So he acted before she finally made up her mind what to do. He knew she was alone in the house. Gavin and Rosie were in the Flints' house and Flint must have seen us from his studio start off on our walk across the fields and guessed we'd be gone for some time."

I thought of Hannah, after her father's murder, sitting in the darkness in her bedroom and telling me that she meant to move away to some remote place, miles from anywhere, where she need never see anyone, and I thought that at that time she had nearly made up her mind to show the photograph to the police and expose Oliver Flint and his motive, then turn her back on the world she knew and disappear. Yet next day she had handed Paul Haycock's letters to her father over to them and exposed what he had done, sooner than risk letting them make a thorough search of the house and find the photograph. It seemed to me that in killing her Oliver Flint had acted sooner than might have been necessary.

"Well, what do we do now?" I asked.

Felix finished his wine. "Go back to the house."

"And then?"

"Think things over."

"What is there to think over? We just hand the photograph over to the police and leave the rest to them."

"There's no hurry about it. I want to be certain it's the right thing to do."

"But what else *can* you do?"

He frowned. "Don't rush me. I only said I wanted to think."

"All right."

We got up and went out, just as the elderly barmaid started calling out, "Time, ladies and gentlemen!"

We hardly spoke as we walked back to the house in the moonlight. Felix had retreated into one of his silences, which there was never any way of penetrating if he did not feel inclined to let one do so. I was a little amused to think that he was in the awkward position of having one of his fantasies turn into reality. He had played the role of the great detective and now he had really found out something of immense importance. The experience evidently bewildered him. His insistence on thinking things over before acting might mean that he was trying to work out how to squeeze the greatest possible drama out of the situation, or it might mean the opposite, that he was wondering how to put the evidence he had into the hands of the police without being involved with them himself.

What I was not prepared for was what he actually did when we reached the house. We had left the door unlocked as Gavin had not thought of giving us a key. Letting ourselves in, we went into the drawing room and Felix immediately drew the curtains, then turned to the fireplace to see if he could stir up a little life in the embers. But the fire had gone out. There was nothing but ash in the grate. Giving up the attempt to waken any small flame, he sat down, took the photograph of Hannah and Oliver Flint out of his wallet, struck a match and held it to the corner of the print.

I would have snatched it from him if it had not flared up so quickly.

"Felix, for God's sake, why did you do that?" I cried. "That's evidence you've destroyed."

He tossed the still burning fragment of paper into the grate.

"And what's so terrible about destroying evidence, if it happens to be inconvenient?" he asked.

"It's a crime, a serious crime."

"But you're the only witness and you can't give evidence against me." He smiled at me. "You're my wife."

"I don't understand what's so inconvenient about it," I said. "Don't you want Oliver convicted?"

"Well, I do and I don't," he answered. "I'd like to think of some way of catching him out without having to produce that photograph. There are Nora and Rosie to think of, you know. You wouldn't want them to see it, would you?"

"Of course not, but I don't want him to go free either. Once you've committed a couple of murders, it'll probably be much easier to commit the third one. The victim might even be Nora, for all you know. I expect she's made a will, leaving him her money. And meanwhile the police may arrest Gavin."

"I asked you not to rush me, didn't I?" he said. "I've got to think things out."

He withdrew into another of his frowning silences.

Presently he got up and crossed the room to the door.

"Where are you going?" I asked.

"Exploring."

"Exploring where?"

"It might be better for you not to know. You get so worked up about things. On the other hand, as I've pointed out to you, you can't give evidence against me. I'm going to Flint's studio. I think the chances are he'll be in the house with the others and the place will be empty and I may be able to break in and find the negative."

"And destroy that too, if you do?"

"Oh yes. My belief is that, now we know who the murderer is, we're certain to be able to find some other evidence against him which will convict him without Nora and Rosie ever having to see that obscene thing. They're going to have enough to bear in any case."

"I suppose what you mean is that you'll fake some evidence to convict him."

"That idea had entered my mind."

"Oh, Felix, when will you grow up? That would be horribly dangerous. And hasn't it occurred to you that the negative has probably been destroyed already? With Hannah and her father dead, Oliver Flint couldn't have made any further use of it and just having it around could be a menace to him."

"I expect you're right, but I think I'll try to make sure."

"Just tell me, have you got some idea already of how you're going to fake evidence against him?"

"Not a trace of one, but I'll think of something. Logically, I feel, there must be more than one way of showing that an event has taken place. Very few things have a single cause. Now get yourself a drink and wait quietly. I don't expect I'll be long."

I did not feel like another drink and when he was gone the

house felt unpleasantly silent and empty. The sense of emptiness was the kind that presses upon one, as obtrusive as any noise. Though the room was not cold, I did not take off my coat but sat huddled in it beside the dead fire.

I wished that I was in a hotel in Spellbridge. Felix's folly appalled me. I supposed that I might have tried harder than I had to check him, but I had found out so long ago how impossible it was to deflect him once he had made up his mind on a course of action that I had not put any real effort into it.

I did not believe that he could successfully forge evidence against Oliver Flint without getting into serious trouble himself. In fact, I did not really believe that Felix intended to do so. I thought that if he found the negative of the photograph that he had burnt he might use it to frighten Oliver Flint and make him vanish out of the lives of Nora and Rosie, but that did not mean that someone else, at some later date, might not be in terrible danger from him. Murder, as we all know, can become addictive. But Felix was never inclined to look ahead very far. His own habit of living from day to day seemed to him perfectly acceptable and he deeply disliked being forced to think about the consequences of his actions.

He was gone longer than I had expected, long enough for me to begin to feel anxious that something had gone wrong and that he was already in trouble. He might have been hunting about the studio when Oliver Flint had come in and caught him. If that had happened, could Felix have been his third victim? In the mood that I was in, it did not seem at all impossible. When the front doorbell rang I had a moment of terror that this was not Felix returning but Oliver Flint, that ogre, come to add a fourth murder to his score. Before opening the door, I slipped the chain into place, opened the door only an inch and asked, "Who's there?"

"Me," Felix answered impatiently.

I unhooked the chain and he came in, looking intensely irritated.

Strolling into the drawing room, he said, "Will you tell me, what's the use of imagination? What's the use of using one's brains? What's the point of having rather more perception than most people if it isn't to make one a little quicker off the mark than the oafs who haven't got any? Why was one given these things if they're never of any use?"

"Haven't you got the negative?" I asked.

"Oh yes, I've got that," he answered indifferently. He took a small negative out of his pocket and, as he had with the print, set a match to it and as it flared tossed it into the fireplace. I did not even think of trying to stop him this time. "I found it at once in one of his files. The thing was hardly hidden. But the place was crawling with police and I thought in case someone had seen me arrive I'd better go into the house and say I'd come to ask how everyone was. That's why I've been so long."

"What were the police doing there? They haven't arrested Gavin?"

"Gavin!" he said contemptuously. "No, they've arrested Flint."

He seemed really put out about it. Groping for a cigarette, he lit it and hurled the match angrily into the fireplace.

I said, "But what's wrong with that? If they've done it without finding the negative, isn't it all to the good? But what evidence have they got?"

He threw himself down in a chair and said disgustedly, "Evidence! They've got witnesses, that's what they've got. They haven't had to use their imagination, or their intelligence, or their understanding of people. They haven't built the truth up, little by little, as I have, by interpreting the odd scraps of information that came my way. They simply had the luck to pick up a couple of people who told them they'd practically seen the whole thing."

"Bruno?" I said.

"He was the first one. He was in the house, of course, when

the first murder happened. He was in the dining room, packing up the silver, when he heard someone come in by the back door. If Flint had come to the front door, he'd have seen Pete's car and probably gone away, but as it was he sneaked in at the back and went straight to Hannah's room without seeing Pete, who'd hidden behind a curtain. Then Pete heard Brownlow come downstairs and the quarrel and the struggle and a great yell from Brownlow. Then Flint got out fast and Pete went along the passage to see what had happened and found Brownlow dead. And looking out of the kitchen window, he saw a man running away and his description of him fits Flint. Pete got out fast himself then, and he got the idea that if he disposed of the silver fast, before the word of the murder got around, and then disappeared for a time, he might get away with it. He didn't, of course, and this afternoon he made up his mind to tell the police what he'd seen because he thought they might not lean on him too hard about the silver if he told them what he knew about the murder."

"Who was the other witness?"

"The Flints' man, who was working in one of their fields when we went for our walk. Flint didn't think he could be seen from where the man was, but he'd moved while Flint was here and the man saw him leave by the back door and make for the studio, and he was sure Flint had blood on the mack he was wearing. But the good man's mind moved slowly and he didn't decide what to do about it till he'd been home and talked to his wife. She told him to go to the police and finally he went to the man in Charlwood and told him what he'd seen. So then the police went along to the Flints' house, found a bloodstained mack in the studio and arrested Flint. That's all. Not what I'd call detection at all."

"Just normal, reasonable police work," I said. "Didn't you say yourself that logically there must be more ways than one of proving that an event has taken place? Their way just happens to be different from yours. But what's Flint's motive supposed to have been?"

"You don't have to prove a motive to get a man convicted of murder," Felix answered. "At the moment the only one they've dreamt up is that Flint was furious with Brownlow because of that block of flats that was going to go up and spoil his view and went to the house to look for evidence of Brownlow's bribery of Haycock, which he'd somehow got to know about, hoping to put a spoke in Brownlow's wheel. Thin, very thin, and ridiculous, of course. Flint didn't give a damn about the flats, because he and Nora were going to move to Portugal. But those witnesses and the bloodstained mack will finish him."

"You ought to be glad," I said. "Nora and Rosie, not to mention Gavin, will never see the photograph, yet Oliver won't go free. You're spared the responsibility of making any decision about it."

"There's that, of course." Felix was always thankful to be spared responsibility. "All the same, I hope you understand my feelings."

"I think I do. You're the frustrated artist. I'm sorry it hurts. But if I were you I'd stick to selling houses. It's more impersonal. What are you going to do now? Go home to-morrow?"

"Are you?"

"If the police don't want us, though I suppose we'll have to come back for the inquest."

"You'll be driving straight home, won't you?" he said. "I'll be going to London by train. So will Kay, I expect. I think I'll telephone her in the morning and see if we can travel to-gether. I'll be going to bed now. All this cerebration takes it out of one."

I said that I would go to bed too. We went upstairs, kissed each other good night at the top and went to our rooms.

In the morning Felix brought me a cup of tea, but he did

not linger to talk, and when presently I went downstairs I found that he had braved the horrors of the kitchen in order to make coffee and toast, which he had taken into the dining room. He told me that he had already telephoned the police and made sure that there was no need for us to stay and that he had then telephoned Kay in Paul Haycock's flat and arranged with her that they should travel to London together by the eleven-forty.

"D'you feel like driving me into Spellbridge," he asked, "or shall I phone for a taxi?"

"I'll drive you in," I said. "But we ought to get in touch with Gavin first and tell him we're leaving. We don't want him to come here and simply find an abandoned house."

"Of course not," Felix said. "Will you phone him?"

"All right," I said and as soon as I had finished my coffee I looked for the Flints' telephone number in the directory, dialled it and was answered by Gavin.

He sounded exhausted and confused and, when I tried to tell him that Felix and I were leaving, kept interrupting me to apologize for having dragged us into the situation that we were all in. I did not think that he was really taking in what I was saying and was glad when Rosie took over from him and said very calmly that she hoped that we should meet again when times were better. I thought that there was not much doubt which of the two of them would supply the strength that is needed in any marriage.

While we were talking Felix wandered into the drawing room. I found him there, handling the Steuben owl that had taken his fancy earlier. I knew the acquisitive look on his face. If I had come in a moment later, the owl would have vanished into his pocket.

"No!" I said.

He started slightly, looked at the owl regretfully, then put it back on the mantelpiece.

"Charming thing," he said. "But, after all, I don't much want to be reminded of the last few days."

I left him, hoping that he would not pocket anything else while I was out of the room, and went upstairs to pack my suitcase.

We left the house at about half past ten, drove into Spellbridge, picked up Kay and went on to the station. I did not wait to see them off but when they had got out of the car drove on, leaving them standing side by side, waving after me.

I wondered if I should feel better or worse if I thought there was the slightest chance of a relationship between them lasting. I knew that they understood one another pretty well and thought that at the moment that would be good for both of them. But I had always believed that the only hope for Felix, the only thing that would ever keep him straight, would be marriage to a very rich wife, preferably somewhat of an invalid. He would look after her with the utmost tenderness, while her money would save him from the unpleasant necessity of doing any more hard work. Kay did not fit the bill. But that did not save me from feeling a kind of deep loneliness as I drove off, leaving them together.

I was meaning to drive straight on to the motorway and make my way homewards, but seeing a stationer's which happened to have an empty parking space in front of it, I thought that I would stop there and buy a newspaper, to see if the two murders figured in it and if there was any mention of the fact that a man was helping the police with their enquiries. I was crossing the pavement when I almost collided with a tall, hurrying man who was going to pass on with a word of apology when he stopped and exclaimed, "Mrs. Freer!"

It was Stephen Ledbetter. He lifted his hat.

"A very cold morning," he observed, which it certainly was. His thin face looked pinched with the chill of it. "Are you leaving us?"

"Yes," I said.

"I tried telephoning the house not long ago," he went on, "but got no answer, so I telephoned the Flints and spoke to Gavin. Those poor people, I wish there were something one could do for them, but in the end time is the only thing that can help. Is your husband with you?"

"No," I said, "he's left for London."

"Then you're alone. I wonder, are you in a great hurry to be off, or have you time to stay on for a little and have lunch with me? It would give me great pleasure if you would. I feel that this isn't the best of times to be alone. It's too easy to start brooding over one's own inadequacy and in the end that does no good to anybody."

I said that I had the same feeling and that I would be delighted to have lunch with him. There are times when the company of a kindly, elderly man is very steadying. We headed towards the Golden Fleece, where he told me the roast beef and Yorkshire pudding were excellent.

E. X. FERRARS lives in Oxfordshire. She is the author of nearly forty works of mystery and suspense, including *Experiment with Death, Frog in the Throat, Designs on Life,* and *Witness Before the Fact.* She was recently given a special award by the British Crime Writers Association for continuing excellence in the mystery field.